THE THIRTEENTH PEARL

NANCY is asked to locate a stolen pearl necklace that is unusual and very valuable. She soon learns that strange and dangerous people are responsible for the theft. They harass her at home and intensify it when she and her father go to Japan, and they finally manage to kidnap Nancy and her friend Ned Nickerson when she returns to River Heights.

Through clever sleuthing, Nancy is able to penetrate the rites of an amazing group of pearl worshippers, some of whose members are far from devout, and she uncovers underhanded dealings of certain employees of World Wide Gems, Inc., a tremendous international jewelry company. Readers will love accompanying Nancy, disguised as a Japanese girl, in this adventure in Tokyo.

"It's some kind of weird cult!" Nancy whispered.

NANCY DREW MYSTERY STORIES®

The Thirteenth Pearl

BY CAROLYN KEENE

PUBLISHERS *Grosset & Dunlap* NEW YORK

A FILMWAYS COMPANY

Contents

The Thirteenth Pearl

CHAPTER I

Mr. Moto

"How would you girls like a drink of pearl powder?" Nancy Drew asked her friends Bess and George. "It's calcium and is guaranteed to cure anything that's wrong with you."

The two girls laughed, sure that Nancy was joking. The attractive, blue-eyed, strawberry blond sleuth shook her head.

"I'm not kidding. It's true."

Bess, a slightly overweight blond who, like the others, was eighteen years old, made a face. "You know how I like to eat, but powder made from pearls!"

George, to whom food meant little, was a slender athletic-looking brunette. "So far as I know, there's nothing wrong with me, so I'll pass."

"Well, Nancy," Bess urged, "tell us what the joke is."

Once more Nancy insisted that pearl powder had been used extensively as a cure-all. "In ancient Japan and other Asiatic and Oriental countries, it was very popular. Nowadays physicians prescribe other medications, but pearl powder can still be purchased in certain pharmacies."

George stopped smiling and looked intently at her friend. "My guess is that you've started working on a new mystery, and it has something to do with pearls. Am I right?"

"Yes," Nancy replied. "There's a Japanese jeweler in town who's a specialist in repairing fine old pieces of jewelry. His name is Mr. Moto. Recently he came to my Dad asking for help on a mystery."

Bess spoke up. "But your dad isn't a detective. He's a lawyer."

"True," Nancy agreed, "but in this case, a fantastic theft took place. Mr. Moto didn't want to go to the police because, if the loss became known, he feared it might cause international complications."

George took a deep breath. "I'm hooked. Tell us more."

Nancy told the girls that a large firm with offices all over the world might be involved.

Bess interrupted. "Is this very confidential?"

"Very," Nancy replied. She went on to say that her father was unable to help with the case at the present time and had told Mr. Moto that Nancy was an amateur detective. Mr. Drew had suggested that the three girls start working on the mystery until he could take over.

"What did Mr. Moto say?" Bess asked.

"He agreed."

"Great!" George exclaimed. "When shall we begin?"

"Right now," Nancy replied. "I'll tell Hannah where we're going." She was referring to the Drews' lovely housekeeper, who had acted as a mother to Nancy since she was three years old and her own mother had passed away. At the moment Hannah Gruen was in the kitchen baking a lemon meringue pie, which happened to be Mr. Drew's favorite dessert.

Minutes later the girls drove off in Nancy's sleek blue car to the center of River Heights. As they turned into a side street looking for the jewelry shop, Bess suddenly said, "Oh, there it is. But what's happening?"

Nancy and George gazed at the front door of the shop. A young Asiatic man was racing from the store with a pearl necklace dangling from one hand.

"I'll bet he's a thief!" George cried out. "Let's nab him!"

But by the time Nancy stopped her car at the curb across from the jeweler's, the young man had jumped into an automobile and sped off in the opposite direction. Unfortunately, the car had

"*I'll bet he's a thief!*" George cried out.

been too far away for Nancy and the others to glimpse the number on the license plate.

"Oh dear!" Bess said with a sigh. "There was our chance to be heroines, and we lost it!"

Nancy was eager to see if Mr. Moto was all right and hurried across the street into the shop. Bess and George followed. No one was inside, but in a few moments an elderly, kind-looking Japanese man came from a rear room.

He smiled and bowed to the girls. "May I assist you?" he asked.

Nancy spoke quickly. "We just saw a young man run from your shop with a pearl necklace in his hand. Did he buy it?"

"No. I have been in the back room. I did not see or hear anyone."

He looked into a display case, then clasped his hands in dismay. "It is gone! A very expensive necklace!"

Nancy, Bess, and George described the young man as best as they could. Mr. Moto did not recognize him.

"He was a thief, indeed!" the jeweler lamented.

The girls expressed their sympathy, and Nancy asked Mr. Moto if he was going to call the police. The rather frail-looking jeweler shook his head. "Not now. I have a bigger problem on my mind."

"I know," Nancy said and introduced herself and the other girls. "You came to see my father about the theft of an unusual piece of jewelry. He told you that until he is free, we would work on your case."

Mr. Moto frowned. The girls assumed that he was thinking, "What do they know about solving mysteries?"

Bess spoke up at once and glibly told how many cases Nancy had successfully concluded. "And sometimes George and I helped her," she added.

Mr. Moto stroked his chin. "Ah, so. Then I will tell you about my trouble. But you must promise to keep this matter to yourselves."

Each girl said she would honor his secret.

"I have a client named Mrs. Tanya Rossmeyer," the jeweler began. "She is a very wealthy lady and owns a great deal of expensive jewelry. Her most precious piece is a necklace of pearls. There are twelve on each side of a very large one, which has the luster of the moon. The strand is made of natural, not cultured pearls."

"It must be worth a fortune!" Bess burst out.

"It is," Mr. Moto agreed. "I believe there is no other one like it in the world."

Nancy asked him about the theft.

"Someone entered my shop and opened the safe," Mr. Moto replied. "He cut off the thirteenth pearl from the rest of the strand. Mrs. Rossmeyer will be very angry and sue me for a lot of money. I will lose my insurance and will be forced to close my shop!"

The three girls were surprised that the burglar had cut only one pearl from the necklace. How much easier it would have been to steal the whole thing!

Nancy said, "Would you let us see the part of the necklace that you still have?"

The jeweler obligingly opened the safe, which was built into the counter and was well-hidden from view.

Nancy thought, "A casual customer would not realize this is a safe. The thief must have been somebody who knows about it, besides being an expert safe-cracker."

Mr. Moto twirled the dials of the lock left and right, then opened the heavy door. Inside were many small drawers. He pulled one out and reached in for the pearl necklace.

"You see where—" he began, then stared at the strand before him. Finally he cried out, "This is not Mrs. Rossmeyer's necklace! The thief substituted this one! These are smaller than Mrs. Rossmeyer's pearls. Oh—she—"

The jeweler suddenly put a hand in his pocket, then fainted, sinking to the floor. The girls ran behind the counter. Nancy and Bess picked him up and carried him to the back room.

"George, shut the front door and lock it!" Nancy called out.

After putting Mr. Moto on a couch, she felt in his pocket where he had put his hand, and she discovered a small bottle of heart tablets. Quickly she placed one under the man's tongue.

"Don't you think we should call a doctor?" Bess asked worriedly.

Nancy thought that Mr. Moto probably had attacks like this from time to time and carried the special pills for that reason. "If he doesn't revive in a few minutes, then we'd better call an ambulance."

George had locked the front door and had gone behind the counter. She restored the pearl necklace to the safe and closed the heavy door. Then she twirled the knob back and forth and tried the handle. The safe was locked.

By this time Mr. Moto had recovered in the back room but was glad to lie on the couch. He insisted he did not need a doctor but asked the girls not to leave him for a while.

George reported that she had locked everything, and he thanked her. "You are most kind," he said. "When I first noticed that the thirteenth pearl was gone, I was so excited that I did not examine the rest of the necklace. Now I know the substitute is not nearly as valuable as the stolen one. Oh, oh! What shall I do?"

Nancy suggested that Mr. Moto lie still until he felt completely well. He agreed and used this time to tell them the full story of what he suspected had happened.

"I believe the thief who was here is working

for an international organization called World Wide Gems, Incorporated, which deals in old and rare jewelry. Recently it has been hinted in the trade that an underworld organization has infiltrated World Wide Gems. This does not mean that the whole company is dishonest, but it is felt that certain employees are not above stealing. No one dares accuse World Wide Gems, since it might stir up real trouble and even cause bloodshed at the hands of the powerful underworld group."

"But why did the thief leave the substitute necklace?" George asked, puzzled.

"Probably he did not want to leave that compartment in my safe empty. With the other necklace in it, I might not have noticed the loss for a while," Mr. Moto replied.

"Where is World Wide Gems located?" Nancy inquired.

"They have branches in many big cities all over the world," Mr. Moto replied. "You can see that an investigation of them would cause many problems."

"Yes, it would," came the stern voice of an unseen man. "You'd better forget the whole thing if you value your life!"

Mr. Moto and the girls were startled. Nancy and her friends jumped up and ran to the back door from where the voice had seemed to originate. No one was there! Puzzled, they searched the premises inside and out, but in vain. It was as if a ghost had spoken.

Bess shivered. "This is positively spooky!"

CHAPTER II

Hidden Camera

THE three girls rejoined Mr. Moto, who had turned very pale. Nancy was afraid he might have another attack. She suggested that he stay on the couch while the girls made a further search for the person who had spoken.

He agreed but said he did not want to close the shop. "With these losses I cannot afford to prevent customers from coming in," he explained worriedly.

Bess offered to work in the store for him. "I would enjoy selling somebody a diamond engagement ring or a wedding ring," she said, her eyes twinkling.

The jeweler smiled faintly. "Some time ago I had a special camera put in to take pictures of anyone who seemed suspicious. This neighborhood is not as high-class as it used to be, and sometimes I have dishonest people coming in."

He got up and showed Bess where the camera was located in a corner of the ceiling. It pointed directly toward the counter.

"There is a button under the counter," he said. "If you press it, the camera will take a picture instantly and develop it. See, here it is."

Bess nodded, sat down on a high stool behind the counter, and gazed at the display before her. Mr. Moto went to lie down again, and when Bess looked at him a few minutes later, he was sound asleep. She smiled and returned to the shop.

Meanwhile, Nancy and George had gone to hunt for the source of the voice. They could find no shoe prints of the eavesdropper and no noticeable fingerprints.

George walked up the driveway between Moto's shop and the next store and questioned pedestrians on the street. None had seen anyone entering or leaving the alleyway. Then she asked people if a man had lingered near the jewelry shop. In each case, the answer was no.

Nancy inquired in apartments above the stores. Most of the tenants were apparently out because they did not answer their doorbells. The few who were home had seen nothing.

She returned to the rear of the jewelry shop. When Nancy looked up, she noticed a young woman leaning out of a window.

Nancy called up to her, "Did you by any chance see a man loitering around Mr. Moto's place?"

"When?" the woman asked.

"Oh, a little while ago, about twenty minutes," the young sleuth replied.

"Yes. A fellow was standing by the back door. He spoke to someone inside."

"He must be the one," Nancy said. "What did he look like?"

The neighbor said she could not see him too well from upstairs. "He was rather short and stocky, had very black hair, and wore a gray suit. I'm afraid that's all I can tell you."

"It's a wonderful identification." Nancy smiled. "By the way, was he of Asiatic origin?"

The woman shook her head. "I couldn't see his face, but I don't think he was." She asked if something was wrong.

Nancy replied that the man had called into the shop, then disappeared. This answer seemed to satisfy the woman, and Nancy was glad she did not have to go into further details.

The young sleuth now turned up the driveway and met George in the street. "Any luck?" she asked.

"None," George replied. "How about you?"

Nancy told her about the clue she had just picked up. Then the girls began questioning passers-by, but no one had seen the mysterious stranger. The two sleuths were about to give up when they saw a woman with a large package walking toward a parked sedan.

To Nancy's inquiry, she answered, "Yes, a man fitting that description ran up the alleyway just as I parked my car."

"Did you see his face?" George inquired. "Can you tell us what nationality he was?"

The woman smiled. "He appeared to be of Italian descent."

Nancy and George were thrilled by this additional information. Now they had something to work on!

"Did you see where the man went?" George asked as she helped the woman put her package into the car.

"Yes. He jumped into a black sedan that somebody else was driving, and they sped off in a hurry."

"Thank you very much," Nancy said. "We're trying to locate this man, and your information will help."

Before the stranger could become inquisitive, the girls turned and walked to the rear of the shop again, letting themselves in through the back door.

Meanwhile, Bess had had an adventure of her own. A rather large, mannish-looking woman with an abundance of blond hair exaggeratedly coiffed had briskly walked into the store. She came up to the counter and said in a harsh voice, "Please give me Mrs. Rossmeyer's address in Europe."

Bess did not like her customer. She seemed hard and cruel. "I don't know the address," the girl replied.

"Oh, come now," the woman said. "If you work here, you certainly must know what address Mrs. Rossmeyer left with Mr. Moto. She's in Europe somewhere. I'm a friend of hers and am going abroad. I want to look her up."

"I'm really sorry," Bess replied, "but I truly don't know it. Why don't you come back some other time and talk to Mr. Moto?"

The stranger was annoyed. "Where is Mr. Moto? Get him. He'll give it to me."

Bess was beginning to worry. The woman did not look or act like a nice person, and she felt that giving her any further information might not be in the best interest of either Mrs. Rossmeyer or Mr. Moto.

She said, "Please come back another day, perhaps tomorrow."

"But I must have the address today!" the woman insisted.

Bess was not sure she knew how to handle the situation. Finally she said, "I'll tell Mr. Moto you were here. What's your name?"

The stranger grew red in the face with anger. "That's none of your business!"

"She's not honest," Bess thought frantically. "She's trying to hide something!" With trembling fingers, the girl reached under the counter and pushed the button that operated the camera on the ceiling.

Trying hard to conceal her nervousness, Bess said, "If you won't leave your name, what shall I tell Mr. Moto?"

"Never mind. But you'll be sorry for your stubbornness, you silly girl!"

With this, the woman turned and hurried out the door. For a moment, Bess stared after her, shocked and surprised. Then she sank down on the stool, trembling.

Just then Nancy and George returned. Having found Mr. Moto sleeping, they tiptoed through the back room into the shop.

"Oh, am I ever glad to see you!" Bess said, her voice shaking.

"What's the matter?" George asked, alarmed.

Bess poured out her story. When she told about taking the woman's photograph, Nancy said, "Good for you! Maybe the police can identify this person. From what you say, I doubt that she's really a friend of Mrs. Rossmeyer's."

The other girls agreed. Bess looked toward the camera. "Who's going to climb up there and get the picture?"

George seemed the most likely candidate. But try as she would, she was unable to reach the camera. At this moment Mr. Moto walked into the shop. He looked refreshed, and color had come back to his face. He gazed up at George, who was stepping on one shelf and trying to reach another.

"What—what are you doing?" he asked in a puzzled voice.

"Bess took a picture of a woman who claimed to be a friend of Mrs. Rossmeyer's. How do you get it?"

Mr. Moto smiled. "I will bring a ladder." He disappeared into the back room and, in a few seconds, returned with a tall, narrow ladder. It had a hook at the end that fitted over the shelf beneath the camera.

"Push that lever on the right," he directed. "The picture will come out the front."

George did this, and a photo appeared. She pulled it out, then descended the ladder. She laid the snapshot on the counter, and they all gazed at it.

"It's an excellent likeness," Bess remarked.

Mr. Moto said, "I do not recognize the woman. You say that she claimed to be a friend of Mrs. Rossmeyer's?"

"Yes," Bess replied, and explained what had happened. "But I don't believe she was telling the truth. She was horrid."

"I do not like this," Mr. Moto said, visibly disturbed.

Nancy asked the jeweler to tell them more about Mrs. Rossmeyer.

"She is a widow," he began, "and travels in European high society. She is not sociable with River Heights people. She has a personal maid, an Asiatic who travels with her. When Mrs. Rossmeyer is at home, her maid does all the shopping, cooking, and so on. There are no other servants."

Nancy felt that Mr. Moto considered the woman a little strange but was too polite to say so.

"I have never seen Mrs. Rossmeyer," he went on. "I only spoke to her over the telephone. The maid brought in the necklace."

"Mr. Moto, would you mind if we take this photograph to the police? It might be a clue to the thief who took Mrs. Rossmeyer's necklace."

Mr. Moto nodded. "But do not say anything about the stolen strand of pearls. I am permitting you to take this picture to the police because Mrs. Rossmeyer's life may be in danger."

As the girls were ready to leave, they extracted a promise from him that he would close up his shop and go home soon.

He smiled. "You are so thoughtful. I appreciate all of this. I believe you will be able to solve my mystery."

"We certainly hope so," Nancy said.

At headquarters it did not take Chief McGinnis long to identify the woman in the photograph.

"Her name is Rosina Caputti," he said, "and

she's the wife of an underworld character known as Benny the Slippery One Caputti."

"What's his specialty?" Nancy asked.

"According to the report, he's a jewel thief."

"Oh!" Bess burst out. It seemed as if she was about to say more, but nudges from Nancy and George made her keep quiet. The three girls wondered if Caputti and his wife were connected with World Wide Gems, Inc.

While Chief McGinnis answered a phone call, Nancy whispered to Bess, "You did a great job today. I think we picked up a very good clue to the mystery!"

CHAPTER III

Sudden Flight

WHEN Chief McGinnis finished his phone call, he looked at Nancy and grinned. "Young lady," he said, "are you getting mixed up with underworld characters?"

The girl smiled back. "Not if I can help it," she replied. "But if there's one for me to catch, you know I'll certainly go after him!"

"Well, watch your step," the officer advised. "The Caputti's are suspected of having committed a number of crimes, but nothing could ever be proved against them."

"I don't want to see that Rosina Caputti again!" Bess declared. "She has a horrible expression on her face, and her eyes bored right through me in Mr. Moto's shop."

Nancy remarked, "You said Caputti is a jewel thief. Does he specialize in pearls?"

"Yes, although he'll take along anything that's handy," the chief replied. "Why do you ask?"

"Because that's what Mr. Moto works with primarily," Nancy replied. "I'd like to find out more about pearls."

"You should call on Professor Joji Mise," Chief McGinnis told her. "He is Japanese and has lived in this country a long time teaching Japanese art. He's a most interesting person, and I'm sure he can give you lots of information about pearls and the customs of his country. Tell the professor I suggested you get in touch with him."

The girls thanked Chief McGinnis and left headquarters.

"Let's call on Professor Mise this afternoon," Nancy suggested as they climbed back into her car. "We can have lunch at my house first."

Bess and George agreed. Later, when they were about to leave the Drew home, Nancy's dog Togo, a frisky bull terrier, barked and whined.

"He wants to come along," said Nancy. "Listen, old fellow, if I take you, will you behave?"

Togo wagged his tail vigorously, which meant that he was promising to be good on the trip. He jumped into the passenger seat in the front, so Bess and George climbed into the rear. When they reached the Mise house, Nancy left Togo in the car and opened the four windows part way for air.

The girls found Professor Mise at home. He

proved to be charming, and his wife a lovely, dainty lady. He considered the police chief a good friend and a very fine officer.

Nancy asked the professor about his native country, and he began to describe Japan, its customs, and some of its history. As he was talking, a large, beautiful tortoise-shell-colored cat wandered into the room, jumped up on the sofa, and settled down to go to sleep.

"What a beautiful animal!" Nancy remarked.

Professor Mise told her that it was a *mike-neko*. "They are a great rarity, and among Japanese fishermen there's a superstition that these cats can make accurate weather forecasts. Japanese sailors often have one or more aboard their vessels. It is even said that they are a charm against shipwreck."

"How interesting!" said Bess, who owned a cat, but admitted it was not as beautiful as this one. Then she requested that the professor tell them something about the history of pearls. "They're only found in the waters of Asia, aren't they?" she asked.

"Oh, no. Pearl oysters live in many parts of the world," the professor replied. "Did you know that even American Indians prized pearls and wore strands of them?"

The girls shook their heads, and their host continued. "Not every tribe did, mostly the ones along the seashore. Indians in Virginia, for instance, liked necklaces, beads, and sometimes even anklets made from pearls."

George spoke up. "How did you find out about this?"

The professor said that it was reported in old documents by white settlers of the 17th century. "Even in Ohio," he went on, "which is not on the ocean, skeletons with pearls in their mouths were found dating back to the era of mound builders."

George raised her eyebrows. "In their mouths?"

"I suppose the Indians believed that the healing propensities of the pearl would be beneficial for the dead person's journey to the happy hunting grounds. You know that the pearl was used for medicinal purposes when that science was still in its infancy. In India, for instance, people used to insert one or more pearls in the wounds of injured warriors to help them heal."

"Do pearls last forever?" Bess asked.

"I do not know about forever, but one pearl found in a Japanese storehouse was a thousand years old. After the dust had been removed, it turned out that the pearl had retained its original luster."

"How marvelous!" Bess exclaimed.

Just then Nancy heard Togo barking. She looked out the window in time to see him leap from the car. He ran to the house and whined to be allowed to come in.

Nancy went to the front door to chastise her pet, but the dog had other ideas. He scooted past her into the living room, where he heard voices. Suddenly he spied the cat on the sofa. He shot across the room and barked furiously at the animal.

The *mike-neko* stood up and arched its back. Togo put his paws on the couch and yapped at the cat. Frightened, it jumped onto a table, knocking over a beautiful Japanese vase. Nancy made a dive for her pet and grabbed him by the collar.

"You naughty, naughty dog!" she exclaimed and took him back to the car. This time she closed the windows a little more so he could not get out again.

She returned to the house and apologized for Togo's actions. "I'm dreadfully sorry about the vase," she said. "May I have it mended or replace it? I would feel much better about this."

Mrs. Mise had taken hold of her cat. She turned to Nancy. "You are not responsible for this mishap. I would not think of permitting you to buy us another one."

Although Nancy was very insistent, her host and hostess would not give in. To help the girl over her embarrassment, the professor went on talking about Japan and pearls.

He mentioned that for thousands of years, people knew only of natural pearls found in oysters. "Then came the industry of pearl culture," he said. "Today it is one of the biggest businesses in Japan. You really should visit that group of beautiful islands and see one of the culture farms."

"Just how are cultured pearls made?" George asked.

"As far as the oyster is concerned, the same way as 'natural' pearls. It happens when a small foreign object gets inside the shell, like a grain of sand, for instance.

"In the pearl beds, man helps this process by inserting a sphere ranging in diameter from two to ten millimeters. These nuclei come from the shell of freshwater bivalves and are polished prior to their use."

"I'll bet the oyster doesn't like that one bit!" Bess declared.

"True. It annoys the oyster so much that it gives off a fluid called nacre. This coats the offending object and hardens. The result is a pearl."

"Then cultured pearls are really not imitations," George said.

"Oh, no. Today that is practically all you can buy because few natural pearls are fished any more. But in ancient times, divers searched the deep water for the oysters. They risked their health, and many times their lives, hunting for pearls, which only royalty and aristocrats were allowed to wear."

"How mean!" Bess said. "That seems very unfair."

Her cousin George could not resist teasing her. "Why Bess, I always thought you wanted to be a queen!"

Bess made a face, but did not comment.

Professor Mise said, "My brother and his wife live just outside Tokyo. If you are ever in Japan, you must look them up. You would be welcome at their home, and my brother, who is retired from government work, would take you to one of the culture farms."

George smiled. "Is it a Japanese custom to invite people to your brother's home?"

The Mises laughed. "In a way, yes," the professor replied. "But we invite only people we like."

"Such a trip would be very exciting," Nancy said. "But right now I can't leave here because I'm working on a case for Mr. Moto, the jeweler."

"Oh, I know Mr. Moto well," the professor said. "A very nice man."

The girls and the Mises talked for a while longer about pearls and Japan, then Nancy and her friends stood up to say good-by.

"Please visit us again soon," Mrs. Mise said. "We will be glad to tell you more about our country."

The girls promised to do so, then thanked their hosts and left.

The following morning, Nancy suggested going to Mr. Moto's shop again. Perhaps he had heard from Mrs. Rossmeyer or had another idea as to who might have stolen her necklace.

When the girls walked through the door, they were surprised to see a stranger standing behind the counter. Nancy inquired about Mr. Moto and was told that the jeweler had left very hurriedly for Japan.

"My name is Kikichi," the man explained. "I am a friend. Mr. Moto asked me to take care of his shop while he is away. May I help you?"

"Did Mr. Moto say *why* he was leaving?" Nancy asked.

"No. He did not."

"Does he have any relatives in Japan?" George asked. "Perhaps it was a family emergency?"

"I do not know. He did not say."

Nancy wondered if by chance the jeweler had received a lead to Mrs. Rossmeyer's stolen necklace and had gone to retrieve it. But why had he not called her?

All three girls felt that Mr. Moto's sudden disappearance was quite strange. Was Mr. Kikichi telling the truth, or was he covering up a secret or foul play?

To verify his story, the girls began looking around the shop, admiring the various art objects. They called back and forth to Mr. Kikichi asking questions and receiving answers.

Nancy drifted toward the back room where Mr. Moto had lain down to sleep the previous day. She wanted to look inside for clues.

As she came closer, Mr. Kikichi called out, "This way. Don't go back there! Come this way!"

Nancy pretended not to hear him and hurried into the room despite his orders. She stopped short in amazement. The place was a shambles!

CHAPTER IV

Rising Sun Insignia

NANCY stared at the disheveled room for a moment, shocked and surprised. Then she retreated silently, waved to Bess and George, and hurried to the front door. With a quick good-by to Mr. Kikichi, who looked angry, the girls left Moto's shop.

Outside, Nancy told what she had seen. "Let's walk around the place. Perhaps we can pick up a clue as to what happened," she suggested.

Two cars were parked in the driveway to the right, and several tire tracks led to the street. Nancy examined them closely. An unusual one caught her eye.

"It has a Rising Sun insignia," she thought. "I wonder whether those tires came from Japan." She checked the tires of the two parked autos, but neither had treads with a Rising Sun mark.

The young sleuth showed Bess and George what she had found. "The tracks are still clear. I wonder if the person whose car made them knows Mr. Moto and gave him a ride?"

She followed the tracks down the driveway until they ended in the street. Here there were so many criss-crossing marks that it was impossible to tell which way the car with the Rising Sun tires had gone.

Disappointed, Nancy returned to the shop. She asked Mr. Kikichi if he knew anyone who owned a car with Japanese tires. He shook his head. "No. Why?"

She did not answer. Instead she said, "Mr. Moto was gone by the time you arrived here this morning?"

"Yes."

"And the back room was a mess when you came?"

"Yes."

"Don't you think that's rather unusual? Mr. Moto was a very neat man. He never would have left his place looking like that."

"You mean," said Mr. Kikichi, "that you suspect foul play? If so, why would Mr. Moto have telephoned me about his plans?"

Nancy said she did not know, but possibly something had happened to him afterwards.

"When did he call you?" she inquired.

"Yesterday. I had just finished dinner."

"I'll go outside and ask people in the area if they saw anyone here last night or very early this morning," Nancy told him.

Bess and George, meanwhile, had walked up and down the street, waiting for Nancy. When she did not reappear, they continued searching for clues.

By this time, Nancy had left Mr. Moto's shop through the back door, trying to find someone to ask about the jeweler. She noticed the neighbor from upstairs to whom she had spoken the day before. The woman was about to cross the street.

Nancy hurried toward her and asked if she had been aware of any disturbance in Mr. Moto's place the previous night.

"No," the neighbor replied. She added with a laugh, "Once my husband goes to sleep, I can't hear anything but his snoring. Why, is something wrong?"

"I don't know," the young sleuth replied. "Mr. Moto left very suddenly for Japan."

"That's strange," said the woman, who introduced herself as Mrs. Rooney. "I was speaking to him just the other day and asked him if he had any intention of visiting his homeland. He said no, not for a while. He was going to wait until he retired in a few years."

"Does he have any family in Japan?" Nancy asked.

"Yes, a brother, Tetsuo, who lives in Tokyo.

Mr. Moto told me about him many times. He's a widower and has visited the United States twice."

Nancy thanked Mrs. Rooney and went to look for Bess and George. She found them a few minutes later.

George held a pair of men's Japanese sandals in her hands.

"Where did you get these?" Nancy asked.

"We found them under a bush next to the driveway," George said.

"I wonder if they belong to Mr. Moto," Bess said.

Nancy examined the leather sandals. "They are quite large," she said. "And Mr. Moto is a small man."

"Let's ask Mr. Kikichi," George declared. "They might belong to him, even though he's not a tall person, either."

The girls went back into the shop and showed their find to Mr. Moto's friend. "Oh, no," he said. "These do not belong to me, and they would not fit Mr. Moto. Not many Japanese have large feet like this!"

A customer walked in at that moment, and Mr. Kikichi went to help her. Bess, George, and Nancy walked outside again.

"What are you going to do with those sandals?" Bess asked Nancy.

"I'm holding on to them for a while," Nancy said. "I have a hunch they might be a clue." She put them in her car, then told her friends what she had learned from Mrs. Rooney.

"I don't believe Mr. Moto went to Japan to visit his brother without planning this ahead," George said after hearing the story.

Nancy nodded. "I'm afraid he may have been kidnapped!"

Bess and George agreed. "The fact that he didn't call Nancy or her father after he had asked them for help just a day or so before is very suspicious," George declared.

"That, and the messed up room," Bess added. "Do you think we should tell Chief McGinnis about this, Nancy?"

"Yes, but first I'll get in touch with Dad. Maybe he'll have an idea."

Bess sighed. "This is becoming too much for me. Stolen jewels, missing persons, a possible kidnapping! I want no part of it."

"For the time being, you'll get your wish," George said, glancing at her watch. "We promised your mother we would take her shopping. Did you forget?"

"I'll drive you home," Nancy offered.

"Oh, no. We'll walk," Bess said. "It isn't far. You go back to your sleuthing so you'll be all finished when we see you later."

Nancy grinned. "I doubt that I'll be that lucky."

As the girls walked off, she decided to talk to

Mr. Kikichi again. "He must be wondering what we were doing there and why we asked so many questions," she thought.

When she entered the shop, he emerged from the back room. "I was locking the rear door," he announced. "What do you wish?"

"I wanted to tell you that I'm trying to find a clue to who might have come in here last night and wrecked Mr. Moto's room," Nancy explained to him.

"I see," said Mr. Kikichi. He looked at her but made no comment except to say that he would straighten up the room when he had a chance.

Nancy promised she would be in touch with him in case she heard from Mr. Moto, then left.

She drove to her father's office and told him what she had seen.

"It certainly appears suspicious," he agreed. "It's possible there was foul play, and Mr. Moto was taken to Japan by force. I'll get in touch with the airlines and see what I can find out. If they have no record of his leaving, I'll contact other likely airports. I'll also check on Mr. Kikichi and notify the police."

Nancy said good-by to her father, but did not go home. Instead, she decided to follow up the clue of the Rising Sun tire. She went to a large garage and asked the manager if people in town used tires with that symbol.

"No," the man replied. "I know of only one person in River Heights who does. I guess he imports them from Japan."

"Is he American or Japanese?" Nancy asked with increasing enthusiasm.

"Oh, he's Japanese, but he lives in this country. For some time now he has had a home on the outskirts of town. I understand he travels to Japan a lot, though."

Nancy was elated. "Do you know his name?"

"Yes. Mr. Kampura."

Nancy thanked the man and went to a public telephone booth to consult the directory. To her disappointment, Mr. Kampura was not listed.

The young sleuth drove back to her father's office and told him what she had found out. Mr. Drew called Chief McGinnis and asked if he knew Mr. Kampura.

"Not personally," the officer replied. "But I understand he has rented a place outside of town."

"What business is he in?" the lawyer inquired.

"He's in the wholesale jewelry business. I believe he works for World Wide Gems, Inc. If you want to contact him, you'd better hurry. He's leaving the United States on Thursday."

Nancy had overheard the conversation. "You know, Dad," she said excitedly, "it appears as if all our leads point to Japan!"

Her father smiled. "You're right. Especially since I've found out that the World Wide Gems headquarters are in Tokyo!"

"Oh, Dad—"

"I know. You want to go there—"

"Yes! On the same flight that Mr. Kampura is taking!"

"Let me think about this for a moment." Mr. Drew went outside to speak to his secretary, then returned, smiling. "I just checked on a few things. I have several business clients in Tokyo, and it might not be a bad idea to see them personally. We could—"

"Oh, Dad, you're wonderful!" Nancy jumped up and gave her father a big hug. "Perhaps Professor Mise could call his brother and tell him we're coming!"

"Good idea. You get in touch with him, and I'll take care of the reservations. Then you'd better pack your wardrobe, and lay out some things for me that you think I might need."

Excited, Nancy drove home and told Hannah Gruen about the proposed trip.

"My, my," said Hannah. "You certainly do get around solving mysteries. This latest one is in beautiful Japan?"

Nancy laughed. "I don't know whether I'll find the solution there, but it's where all my clues lead to. I'm really worried about Mr. Moto."

The kindly housekeeper said she was glad Nancy and her father were leaving. "With underworld characters here who might have harmed Mr. Moto, I think it's a good idea that you're going out of town."

Nancy phoned Professor Mise to tell him the news. A half hour later he called back and said he had telephoned his brother and that Toshio Mise and his wife would be happy to have the Drews as guests in their home, and they would pick them up at the airport.

Nancy passed the message on to her father when he came home.

"That's extremely nice of the Mises," he said. "I hope we'll be able to repay them somehow for their hospitality."

"Have you any news on Mr. Moto?" Nancy inquired hopefully.

"He didn't fly out of any of the coastal airports, at least not under his own name. But if he was kidnapped and taken to Japan, I'm sure his abductors provided a fake passport."

"Which would make it even harder for us," Nancy said. "Oh, I do hope we find out what happened to him."

When Nancy and her father reached the airport in New York on Thursday, he said, "How do you propose to identify Mr. Kampura? There might be many Japanese on board our plane."

A sudden idea came to Nancy. "Let's have him paged and wait near the check-in counter. When he shows up, we can see what he looks like."

Her father agreed, stepped up to the desk, and put in the request. Then he and Nancy walked out of sight, but watched the counter carefully from a distance.

Soon a Japanese man arrived to answer the call. He was about six feet tall, slender, and had a severe, square-jawed face. He reminded Nancy of Genghis Khan's cruel raiders of ancient times.

Mr. Drew turned to his daughter and whispered, "Nancy, don't ever tangle with him!"

The Drews hurried away before Kampura could learn that the call was a fake. "Dad," Nancy said, "remember I told you about the sandals Bess and George found in Mr. Moto's driveway?"

"Yes."

"They were rather large for a Japanese man, yet they were made in Japan."

"Many sandals are."

"But these were not the kind usually sold in our country."

"I see what you mean. You think they might belong to Mr. Kampura because he's very tall?"

"Yes! Between the sandals and the tire tracks with the Rising Sun insignia, I'm convinced Mr. Kampura was in Mr. Moto's shop recently!"

"I'm inclined to agree," Mr. Drew said.

Just then a message came over the loudspeaker.

"Will Mr. Campbell Drewry please go to the nearest phone?"

Nancy's father winked at her and headed for a booth. The girl was puzzled. Slowly she followed her father and watched him pick up the receiver. Why had he answered the call?

Suddenly an idea came to Nancy. She recalled that Campbell was her father's middle name, which he never used.

"Clever!" she thought to herself, a smile spreading across her face. "Dad must have instructed his office to use that name in case they had a message for him before he left. This way he could not be identified," Nancy thought. "I wonder what the message is?"

CHAPTER V

Shocking News

"MR. DREWRY" reported to Nancy that his secretary, Miss Hanson, had checked with various other airlines that Mr. Moto might have taken to Japan.

"None of them had any record of a flight booked in his name," he said. "I also got word on Mr. Kikichi. As far as she could ascertain, he's in the United States legally, and there were never any charges against him."

"Thank you for your report, Mr. Campbell Drewry," Nancy said with an impish grin as they walked toward the boarding gate. Mr. Drew squeezed his daughter's left arm affectionately.

"You're welcome. And now we'd better go. Our flight is ready."

The Drews followed a group of passengers onto the large jet and took their seats. Nancy was in-

trigued by the dainty hostesses in native kimonos.
Before the first meal was served, the young
women brought in steaming hot towels for the
passengers to wash their hands with. When the
trays of food were set before them, the Drews
looked at them, wondering how they would enjoy the exotic dishes.

Nancy remarked politely, "Isn't that an attractive color arrangement?" The tray contained
a bouquet of green parsley in a small vase. Next
to it was a tiny platter with pinkish raw fish.
White boiled rice and a dish of broiled eel were
alongside it. A pot of green tea was served, and
dessert consisted of a combination of fresh apri-
cots and peaches.

Mr. Kampura was seated at the very front of
the plane near the exit door. Once Mr. Drew
walked up close to him and talked to the hostess,
but he kept his eyes on the Japanese man all the
while. Kampura was speaking to the man sitting
next to him, but their conversation was unintel-
ligible to the lawyer.

When they arrived at their destination many
hours later, Mr. Kampura was the first to get off
the plane. Nancy and her father tried to follow
him, but with most of the passengers standing in
the aisle, it was impossible.

The Drews claimed their baggage and walked
out into the lobby. They noticed a Japanese
couple who were waiting near an exit. The man

looked so much like Professor Mise in River Heights that Nancy and her father felt he must be his brother.

The Americans walked up to the couple.

"Pardon me, but are you Mr. and Mrs. Mise?" Nancy asked.

The man smiled. "Ah, yes. And you are Mr. Drew and Miss Nancy Drew?"

"Yes, we are," the lawyer replied. "We're delighted that you speak English. Unfortunately, we have never learned your language."

The couple bowed low to the visitors, and Mr. Mise said, "You make us very happy by visiting us. Perhaps you will pick up some Japanese phrases while you are here."

"I'd like to," said Nancy.

Mr. Mise took her suitcase, and the Drews followed their hosts outside to a waiting car. Nancy could not resist taking a peek at the tires. They did not have the Rising Sun insignia on them.

As Mr. Mise drove through the city, Nancy and her father commented how much it resembled an American metropolis, despite the sprinkling of one-story brown wooden houses, which served as a small reminder of "Old Japan." Most of the people wore Western dress, and the streets were literally teeming with the city's ten million inhabitants.

Mr. Mise came to an open area with a large

marketplace and stopped the car. "Would you like to get out and walk around?" he asked. "This is one of our flower markets. We Japanese like our gardens to be all green because we think it induces tranquility and rest. But we enjoy flowers in the house."

Part of the area was filled with chrysanthemums of every conceivable color and size. These flowers were not yet in full season, and apparently they had been forced.

Mr. Drew spoke up. "May I purchase some for you, Mrs. Mise?"

The woman smiled and bowed. Later Nancy learned that it was considered bad manners for a Japanese to refuse a gift, which was called a *presento*.

Yellow chrysanthemums were bought, then the journey proceeded to the Mises' home, which was several miles out of town. It proved to be a beautiful place and was entirely concealed from the road by trees and bushes. A gardener on a step ladder was pulling needles from a pine tree.

Mrs. Mise explained why. "Japanese do not care for bushy gardens. We like to be able to look through the foliage, so a certain number of needles are pulled out."

They rode to the house. Mrs. Mise, Nancy, and Mr. Drew alighted, while Mr. Mise took the car to the garage. The house was designed in true Japanese style, with sliding panels for walls.

The panels could be opened easily to give more space.

Mrs. Mise said with a smile, "We do not sit on the floor to eat, as many of our countrymen do. We prefer the type of table and chair that you have in your country."

Nancy asked if the couple slept on the floor, as was the custom, and was told that in their second floor bedrooms there was American furniture. Mrs. Mise led the Drews to their rooms, and while the visitors were unpacking clothes, she arranged the chrysanthemums in a typical Japanese pattern. At the top of the bouquet was one flower, surrounded by leaves. Below it was another, and near the rim of the vase was a third. The arrangement was very artistic.

When Nancy and her father came downstairs and noticed the beautiful bouquet, Mrs. Mise explained that the top flower represented Heaven, the middle one Man, and the lowest one Earth.

At dinner, which was served by a dainty young woman in Japanese costume, conversation turned to the main reason for the Drews' visit. The stolen necklace was not mentioned, but Mrs. Rossmeyer was. The Mises had heard of her through the press, but had never seen the woman.

"We are interested in an organization called World Wide Gems," Mr. Drew told them. "Do you happen to know a Mr. Kampura, who is connected with the company?"

Mr. Mise said, "I have met the man but do not know him well. World Wide Gems has its main office in Tokyo, but the many salesmen are scattered throughout the world."

Nancy asked, "Would it be possible for us to meet Mr. Kampura?"

Mr. Mise thought this could be arranged. He would telephone in the morning to find out.

Now the Drews told the Mises about the missing jeweler, Mr. Moto. "We heard from his friend, Mr. Kikichi, that he had gone to Japan," Nancy explained. "But none of the airlines we asked had issued a ticket to him. We think he might have been kidnapped."

"Oh, no!" Mrs. Mise said. "What are you going to do?"

"He has a brother in Tokyo," Nancy said, "Tetsuo Moto. I would like to find out if Tetsuo has heard from him."

Mr. Mise brought out a telephone directory to find Tetsuo's number. There was a listing, but when he called up, he was told that the number had been disconnected because the man had moved.

"Shall I get in touch with the police and explain the situation?" Mr. Mise asked. "Perhaps they can trace Tetsuo Moto for you."

"That would be a good idea," Mr. Drew said, and the host put in the call.

"The officers will let me know if they can find

him," he reported after a short conversation. "And now it is late. Any time you wish to go to bed, do tell us. We want you to feel at home while you are here. Please do not hesitate to ask us for anything you may desire."

Mr. Drew said, "You are very thoughtful. Nancy and I are tired and would appreciate getting some sleep. Once more I want to thank you for inviting us here."

Nancy spoke up. "Your brother, the professor, and his wife are wonderful people. I can see that you are exactly like them."

Everyone said good-night and went to his room. The following morning when Nancy came to breakfast she found an envelope alongside her plate. Her name was printed on it in large, bold letters. Inside was a single sheet of writing paper containing the following equation:

$$4 + 9 = 13$$

Puzzled, Nancy handed the note to Mr. Mise and asked if he knew what it meant.

A worried expression spread over his face. "Four is *shi* in Japanese, which also stands for death. Nine is *ku*, which translates to suffering in pain. Thirteen has no double meaning."

"It does to me," Nancy said slowly. "I'm sure it refers to the thirteenth pearl."

"I do not understand," Mr. Mise said. "What is the thirteenth pearl?"

"Danger!" Mr. Drew said tensely, then told the Mises about Mrs. Rossmeyer's stolen necklace.

When he finished, their host frowned. "Do you think the stolen thirteenth pearl has been brought to this country?"

"That's what we're trying to find out. We believe that Mr. Kampura might be mixed up in this somehow, and we are here to investigate."

Mrs. Mise had a suggestion. "When you go to Mr. Kampura's office, Nancy should dress like a Japanese girl. Then she will not be recognized if someone is following you."

Mr. Mise thought this was a wise idea. He also felt that he should go with Nancy, while Mr. Drew and his wife should leave later and take a different route.

An appointment with Mr. Kampura had been made for 11:00 o'clock. This left plenty of time for Mrs. Mise to disguise Nancy. The woman said she had been a dancer and knew all about make-up.

"I am sure I can make you look like a Japanese girl."

First she rubbed white salve on Nancy's face and covered it with powder to lighten her sun-tanned skin. Then she darkened and upturned Nancy's eyebrows and put a black wig on her head. It had a tiny lotus blossom on one side. She was given a rosebud-type mouth.

Finally Mrs. Mise brought out a pretty but

subdued kimono, an obi, a pair of white stockings, and sandals. When the young detective was ready, she went downstairs. Her father and Mr. Mise were astounded at the change in her appearance.

"It's a perfect disguise!" Mr. Mise marveled. "I would never recognize you."

Mr. Drew joked about his lovely little Japanese daughter. Then she and Mr. Mise set off in his car. They arrived at the offices of World Wide Gems about ten minutes earlier than Mr. Drew and Mrs. Mise.

Mr. Kampura had a very attractive office furnished partly in Japanese and partly in Western style. Nancy bowed low when she was introduced, but on purpose her name was so slurred that no one could understand it.

Just then a man walked into the room and stopped short when he saw the visitors. "So sorry to interrupt," he said with a smile. "I was not aware that you had guests."

Mr. Kampura seemed uncomfortable at the interruption. "This is Mr. Taro, the president of our organization," he introduced the pleasant-looking Japanese man. "May I present—"

But Mr. Taro, not wishing to disturb the meeting, had already turned and slipped out the door. Nancy breathed a muted sigh of relief, since she did not want her name repeated.

"Nancy, it's a perfect disguise!" Mr. Mise exclaimed.

"What can I do for you?" Mr. Kampura asked, impatience showing in his voice.

"I will be brief," Mr. Drew replied, realizing that Mr. Kampura did not wish his callers to stay long. "I am a lawyer in the United States, and it is important that I find Mrs. Tanya Rossmeyer. I understand she is probably in this country buying jewelry."

Mr. Kampura said nothing, so Mr. Drew went on, "It is essential that I discuss a legal matter with her. I have been told that she has purchased a good bit of jewelry from your company. Can you tell me where she is?"

There was a long pause, then Mr. Kampura said, "Yes, I know of Mrs. Rossmeyer. She was a client of ours. But I believe she was in Europe recently and met a tragic death!"

CHAPTER VI

Conked Out!

FOR several moments after Mr. Kampura's shocking announcement about Mrs. Rossmeyer, there was silence. Nancy and her father looked at each other, then at the Mises.

Finally Mr. Drew asked, "Are you sure of your information? We heard nothing about this in our country."

Mr. Kampura rose from his chair and said, "I have no details. Her death was discussed at a jeweler's conference. As you know, she was a lover of gems and, therefore, was well known to the trade."

"In a company as large and successful as yours," Mr. Drew said, "I suppose you have a good deal of thievery."

"Oh, no, not at all," Mr. Kampura replied. "We have very tight security and little loss." Impatiently, he stepped from behind his desk and went toward the door. The Drews and the Mises realized that he did not wish to prolong the meeting, and they followed him.

"I'm from a rather small town in the United States," Mr. Drew said. "However, a Japanese man lives there who is an expert on gems. His name is Moto. Do you know him?"

"No," Mr. Kampura replied, "I have never heard of him."

He opened the door, and the visitors thanked him, said good-by, and left. No remarks were exchanged as they went down in the elevator and out the building.

When they were seated once more in the Mises' car, Mrs. Mise spoke up. "Nancy, I am sure that Mr. Kampura did not discover your disguise. I am very glad."

"So am I," Nancy remarked. "I have a hunch that Mr. Kampura was not telling the truth about either Mrs. Rossmeyer or Mr. Moto. Let's try to find out about Mrs. Rossmeyer through other sources."

Mr. Mise directed them to a Tokyo newspaper office that published an English edition. They looked through file copies for any notices of the socialite's death. There was nothing, and the group drove home.

Mr. Drew made various overseas telephone calls but could not verify the report that Mr.

Kampura had given them. Finally Nancy had an idea.

"Dad, you remember Renee Marcel who attended school with me? She was from Paris and now is a society reporter for a paper there. Why don't I get in touch with her? Surely if Mrs. Rossmeyer died, Renee would know about it."

"Good thinking. Phone Renee and see what she can find out."

Nancy put in the call and surprised her friend. The two girls chatted about personal matters for a few moments, then Nancy asked about Mrs. Rossmeyer.

"Hold the line," Renee answered. "I will make a quick search." She was gone no more than two minutes. "Nancy," she said upon her return, "this story is not true. Night before last, Mrs. Rossmeyer gave a large dinner party in Paris. I'll try to get in touch with her and let you know more details if I can."

Nancy gave Renee the Mises' telephone number and waited for an answer. It came after lunch.

"I learned that Mrs. Rossmeyer is in good health," Renee reported. "She told a friend that for personal reasons she was going into hiding for a short time."

"Have you any idea where?" Nancy asked.

Renee said that one source had mentioned Japan, another the United States. Later that day, the girl phoned again. She had spoken to the porter in Mrs. Rossmeyer's hotel. He had heard her say the previous day that she was heading for the airport to fly to Japan to the Mikomoto Pearl Farm. It was her expectation to make some large purchases.

Nancy was elated about the news. "Could we go there soon and verify the report?" she asked Mr. Mise.

"It is a long way from here," he said. "But a friend of mine runs a seaplane that he charters to groups. Let me call him and see when the next flight is."

After a short phone conversation, their host hung up with a smile. "The plane is leaving for the pearl farm early tomorrow morning."

"Wonderful!" Nancy exclaimed. "We're in luck!"

Conversation now turned from Mrs. Rossmeyer to Mr. Kampura. Had he lied intentionally to throw the Drews off the scent? Was Mrs. Rossmeyer in some way connected with World Wide Gems? Was he trying to protect her? And why had he denied knowing Mr. Moto? Had they not been his tire tracks that showed the Rising Sun insignia in the rear of the jewelry shop?

Nancy mentioned that she felt it was probably wise to contact the police at this point. "They may have records on World Wide Gems, Mr. Kampura, and Mrs. Rossmeyer."

Mr. Mise said he would take Nancy to headquarters but suggested that perhaps she would like to remove her Japanese disguise.

"I'll be happy to," Nancy said.

It took her nearly half an hour to restore her skin to the American look, to lighten the blackened eyebrows, and to change into her own clothes. Then she and Mr. Mise set off. He knew the chief of police personally and explained their case, translating for Nancy what he learned.

"It is not generally known, but World Wide Gems is under surveillance in several countries," the chief told them. "As you heard in the United States, the organization as a whole is not suspected of any wrongdoing, but certain members are thought to have connections with underworld characters. The police are watching carefully."

"Is Mr. Kampura under suspicion?" Nancy asked.

"Not so far. Why?"

"Because we think that he visited Mr. Moto's jewelry shop in River Heights just before the jeweler disappeared without a trace. But Mr. Kampura denied knowing Mr. Moto. He also told us Mrs. Rossmeyer had a fatal accident, which does not seem to be true."

The chief nodded thoughtfully. "We will try to find out more about Mr. Kampura."

Nancy asked the chief about Mr. Moto, but as far as he knew, the man had not come to Japan.

"I'm afraid he was kidnapped," Nancy said. "It

seems strange that Mr. Kikichi, whom he left in charge of his shop, had not heard anything from his friend after he left."

"It is possible," the officer said, "that Mr. Moto, for some reason of his own, disappeared in a hurry, and therefore left his room in a shambles. Has anyone investigated the possibility that he might have gone into hiding?"

Nancy admitted that they had not thought of this. "But why should he?" she asked. "He has had the shop in River Heights for many years and is highly respected."

"Even the finest people can have enemies," the officer said with a smile. "They might be connected with business, or family, or even friends."

"But Mr. Moto is such a nice man. I can't imagine his having any personal enemies. I'm sure that if something happened to him, it was because of the thievery going on in his business."

The chief promised to let her know if any leads to Mr. Moto's disappearance turned up, and Nancy and Mr. Mise thanked him, then left.

After their visit to police headquarters, there was still enough time for the Drews to do some shopping and to go to Mr. Tetsuo Moto's former residence to see if they could learn a clue from the neighbors.

Mr. Mise picked up Mr. Drew, who had visited a business associate during his daughter's trip to police headquarters, then he drove the Drews to the Ginza, Tokyo's main shopping street. Nancy's first purchase was a lovely pearl necklace for Hannah Gruen. The salesman showed them matching earrings and suggested that the lucky receiver of the necklace could surely use earrings to go with it.

Mr. Drew smiled. "All right, we'll take them for Hannah, too."

Pretty pins of pearls intertwined with enameled leaves were selected for Bess and George. Nancy's gift to Ned Nickerson was a pearl stick pin, and she bought cufflinks for Burt and Dave with money the girls had given her. The Drews concluded their shopping with a lovely pearl and silver bracelet for Mr. Drew's sister, Eloise.

While they were waiting for the articles to be gift-wrapped, Nancy wandered around the store looking at pictures on the walls. Suddenly she stopped in front of an oil painting of a queen. She was wearing a necklace with a huge pinkish pearl in the middle and smaller-sized white ones on both sides of it.

"I wonder if this is like Mrs. Rossmeyer's," Nancy thought and looked at the date of the picture. It was a hundred years old.

"This type of necklace must have been popular with royalty in those days," the girl mused.

Just then Mr. Mise said he would bring the car to the door. After he left, the Drews examined various art objects that were displayed throughout the shop. They saw a vase that was very similar to the one belonging to Professor Mise and his wife in River Heights, which Togo had inadvertently broken.

"Let's buy it and have it sent to them!" Nancy urged her father. He agreed. When the transaction was taken care of, they walked out of the shop and climbed into Mr. Mise's car.

He drove them to the street where Mr. Moto's brother had lived. They found the small apartment building facing one of the many streams that crisscrossed the city.

"Suppose we question the neighbors first," Nancy suggested. "I'll go with Mrs. Mise and Dad with Mr. Mise, so we each have a translator."

"Good idea," Mr. Drew agreed. "We'll meet out here when we're finished."

It was more than an hour before the four assembled in the street again. Their search had been unsuccessful. A number of people had known Tetsuo Moto, but could tell the Drews no more than that he had moved to the country. Next, the group went to all neighborhood stores and questioned the owners, but again in vain. There was no trace of the jeweler's brother!

"We'll just have to rely on the police to track him down," Mr. Drew said to Nancy, who was very disappointed. "I'll call them again tonight."

She nodded. "Even though I believe Mr. Moto was kidnapped, I was still hoping to pick up some

information from his brother, Tetsuo. Well—"
she sighed, "maybe we'll find a clue elsewhere."

Early the following morning the Mises and the
Drews set out for a visit to a pearl farm. They
drove to the dock where the seaplane was an-
chored and joined a group of people for the take-
off. The journey was pleasant and the scenery
interesting, with woods and mountains in the
background.

"Tell me something about pearl farms," Nancy
begged Mr. Mise.

"I will be glad to," he said. "You see, there are
two kinds of beds, those in which the oysters are
raised until they are large enough to be used in
pearl culture, and those in which they are kept
after insertion of the nucleus."

"Today we'll see one of the latter kind, won't
we?" Nancy asked.

"That is right. They must be in an area where
nutritious plankton is plentiful and where the
currents can flow freely around the oyster," Mr.
Mise went on, "but they shouldn't be near mouths
of rivers that pump pollution into the sea."

"Should the water be a certain temperature?"

"Oh, yes. The oysters tolerate a range between
fifty and seventy-seven degrees Fahrenheit. Since
the farm waters reach temperatures below fifty
degrees in the winter, the rafts and baskets must
be moved farther south. To people in the culture

region, these caravans that are pulled by boats
are a familiar sight."

Nancy laughed. "I wonder if the oysters enjoy
the trip."

"I suppose we will never know," Mr. Mise said
with a chuckle.

"How about depth?" Nancy asked. "Does that
influence the production of nacre?"

"Definitely. In shallow water, more layers develop, but they tend to be of inferior quality."

"What is considered shallow?"

"About seven to ten feet. You see, when water
temperatures are between fifty-nine and seventy-
seven degrees in the summer, increased nacre production is encouraged. But in the winter, the
oysters are lowered to a depth of about seventeen
to twenty feet. This insures a lovely pink color
and better quality."

"How old are the oysters when they are in-
jected with the nucleus?" Nancy inquired.

"About two years."

After a long flight, the pilot's voice sounded
over the intercom. He announced that they would
be landing soon. He spoke first in English, then
in Japanese.

Suddenly the seaplane began to lurch.

"What's happening?" Nancy asked apprehen-
sively, looking at her father.

"I don't know," Mr. Drew replied. "I can't
imagine—"

The craft lurched again, and the smooth hum of the engines seemed to change. The passengers were tossed about, and a woman screamed. An engine conked out, then the other. Nancy and her father grabbed each other's hands. Were they about to crash?

CHAPTER VII

Chase in the Park

THERE were tense and fearful moments as the plane descended at a quick rate toward the sea. All passengers were strapped in and put their heads in their laps, awaiting the crash.

But the pilot was skillful. He managed to touch the water lightly, then lifted the craft so it bounced along the shoreline like a stone being tossed across the water.

He finally managed to land safely, and no one was injured. Relieved, the passengers aboard began to talk excitedly.

Mr. and Mrs. Mise congratulated Nancy and her father for having remained so calm. "I can see that you are experienced travelers," Mr. Mise said as the seaplane floated tranquilly to a dock.

"Good thing we didn't crash," Mr. Drew said, "or the pearl-making oysters here would have gotten a dreadful scare!"

The others laughed, then Mr. Mise asked the pilot what had gone wrong and translated the answer.

"He feels that someone tampered with the engines. After a complete examination, he will let us know."

Mr. Drew said he would appreciate this, as his group intended to fly back to Tokyo that same day. "Meanwhile, we'll tour the pearl farm."

A guide took the visitors offshore in a boat, showing them the long bamboo rafts that contained the oyster beds.

"The oysters hang from the rafts in wire-mesh or plastic baskets," he explained. "They feed on plankton and must be cleaned from time to time. We have a crew here that inspects the beds daily. The men must keep an eye on worn or broken ropes and inspect the oysters for disease."

"Who injects the nuclei?" a white-haired Englishman asked.

"That's done by young ladies called *tamaire-san*. Freely translated, that means *Miss Pearl-pusher*," the guard replied with a smile. "The girls open the oysters carefully with a special tool. After the operation, the oysters are allowed to rest for a while in quiet waters about seventeen feet deep."

"It must be quite a shock to their systems," Nancy declared.

"It is, and many eject the nucleus. We have

x-ray equipment that tells us which oysters do, and we do not bother raising those."

"I see some floating buoys way out there," Nancy remarked. "What are they for?"

"Those are experimental glass fiber buoys, roughly one foot in diameter, which will eventually replace wooden or bamboo rafts because they are more durable and economical," the guide replied.

"When are the pearls ready for harvesting?" Mr. Drew inquired.

"They are 'beached' after about two to three years. This takes place in the arid winter when the pearl-sac cells have stopped secreting nacre, and the top layer is completely crystallized."

"I'll bet that's an exciting occasion," Nancy remarked.

"Yes, indeed. The oysters are opened one by one with small knives, and out come pearls in many sizes and different qualities. About twenty percent cannot be used at all, and truly precious pearls are quite rare."

"Can you produce a bigger pearl by inserting a larger nucleus?" a blond woman asked.

"Yes, but that is risky financially because large nuclei kill many oysters."

"I feel sorry for the poor oysters," Nancy said. "For two to three years they are irritated by the foreign object inside them."

"True," the guide admitted. "But then, nature

does the same thing. Man does not harm the oyster any more than nature does."

When their tour was over, Nancy and her father spoke to the manager of the pearl farm and asked if Mrs. Tanya Rossmeyer had visited the Mikimoto Farm.

"No," he said, "and we have not heard from her. However, I will be glad to call you if Mrs. Rossmeyer should visit us."

The Drews thanked the man and gave him the Mises' phone number, then joined the rest of the group for the return flight.

The trip back to Tokyo was uneventful, and they reached the Mises' home in the evening. On the doorstep lay a note addressed to Nancy Drew.

She opened it quickly and held her breath. The familiar $4 + 9 = 13$ equation was the only message. Nancy showed it to the others, then said to her father, "It's not fair to put the Mises in any danger. I think you and I should leave here."

"You mean, go back to the United States?" her father asked.

Before Nancy could reply, both Mr. and Mrs. Mise spoke up. They insisted that their guests stay with them. They were not afraid, and besides, they felt that they could give the Drews some protection.

"Anyway, the person who is sending these threats may forget the whole affair if we do not take him seriously. Meanwhile, I suggest that we get away from the house for more sightseeing," Mr. Mise said.

Nancy and her father did not feel this way about it, but did not object to the idea.

"What do you recommend?" Mr. Drew asked.

"A trip to the famous Nara Park," Mr. Mise said. "It is a lovely place to visit and is full of interesting things to see."

Mrs. Mise smiled. "Nancy, you will love the little deer that come out of the woods and greet tourists."

"Isn't that quite a distance from here?" Nancy inquired.

"Yes, about an hour's flight," Mr. Mise replied. "I will make the reservations right away."

Next morning they drove to the airport and departed for Nara. The town had been Japan's capital in the 8th century, preceding Kyoto and Tokyo. The visitors enjoyed the sights before continuing to the famous park, which was a spectacularly beautiful place. People crowded the entrance and chuckled at the small deer that clustered around them, bowing their heads in welcome.

"Aren't they darling?" Nancy exclaimed. She patted several of the animals, who were very friendly, then followed the Mises on a walk along the paths that meandered among the trees.

They finally came to an enormous statue of

Buddha and gazed at it in awe. The benign figure had its right hand raised as if blessing a congregation. Mr. Drew remarked that it must weigh an enormous amount.

"Five hundred tons," Mr. Mise said. "The total height is seventy-one and a half feet. The Buddha itself is fifty-three feet tall, and the face alone is sixteen feet in height."

"That really is tremendous," Nancy remarked. "When was it cast?"

"In the year seven hundred and forty-nine A.D. It contains several metals, but the outside is bronze."

Nancy asked her host about the main tenets of Buddhism and its great teacher Guatama Buddha.

Mrs. Mise replied, "That suffering is inherent in life, and that one can be liberated from it by mental and moral self-purification."

Nancy thought this over, then said, "If a person could do that, he would be perfect."

"That is true," Mr. Mise said. "Many Buddhist priests try to attain this goal and deny themselves most of the pleasures of life. We, who are not priests, also try to accept pain and to live moral and upright lives."

Nancy smiled. "You are such kind, helpful people. I am sure you're succeeding beautifully."

The couple seemed embarrassed by the compliment and changed the subject. Nancy, meanwhile, had noticed how many people were taking photographs. Most of them were Japanese, but there was a sprinkling of visitors from countries all over the world.

Suddenly she saw a man who was snapping *her* picture. She stared at him and realized that he was short, had black hair, a hard face, and was wearing a gray suit. He looked to be of Italian descent. Could he possibly be Benny the Slippery One Caputti?

When the man became aware that she had spotted him, he turned and hurried around the statue. Nancy took off after him, her camera ready to snap his picture.

By the time she reached the rear of the great monument, the fugitive was running away at a fast clip. Nancy pursued him and was closing the distance between them, when suddenly a guard stepped up and stopped her.

"Please! You must not pursue an innocent man in this holy park!" he said.

Nancy was amazed. What made the guard think that the fleeing man was innocent? Certainly the fact that he was racing away made him highly suspect!

She said, "I don't think that man is innocent. I believe he's wanted by the police!"

Suddenly Nancy realized that the guard had spoken English without the slightest accent, and that he did not look Japanese. Was he a friend of

Caputti's and had he borrowed or stolen the Japanese guard's uniform?

The girl decided to pay no attention to him and started to hurry off. He grabbed her by the shoulders. "Don't you dare run away!" he hissed at her.

CHAPTER VIII

Nancy Accused

NANCY had to make up her mind in a hurry whether to try to get away from the man or turn the tables on him and prove that he had helped a criminal escape.

In the distance she saw her father running in her direction. He had called another guard, who was hurrying along with him.

By the time Nancy's adversary realized that he was about to be caught, he let go of her and started to run. But the girl grabbed his wrist and held on tightly. Tug as he would, he could not get away before Mr. Drew and the other guard had caught up.

"What's going on here?" the lawyer demanded.

Before the suspect could answer, the guard who had accompanied Mr. Drew spoke up. "This

man is not one of us!" He turned to the impostor.
"Who are you?"

The man did not reply, so Nancy told her story
and her suspicion that he was in league with a
man who was wanted by numerous United States
authorities.

"I will take him into custody and hold him
until he talks," the legitimate guard declared.

He asked the impostor where he had obtained
the uniform. The suspect stared defiantly, but
said nothing.

Nancy tried to catch him by surprise. "Where
did Benny Caputti go?" she asked him.

The prisoner jumped and blinked, indicating
that the girl had touched upon a vital subject.
Still he did not talk.

"It is against the law to impersonate an officer,"
the guard declared. "You will have to come
with me!"

Suddenly the suspect cried out, "Why don't
you arrest this girl? She molested a visitor, trying
to photograph him against his will. See her camera? She was bothering people with it."

Nancy and her father were startled, but Nancy
said calmly, "He's trying to twist things around.
The fellow who fled, and who I believe is in
league with this man, took *my* photograph. That's
why I chased him."

The guard nodded and handcuffed the prisoner. "I understand. Just give me your names and addresses in case the police want to contact you."

The Drews did, but before leaving Nara, they went to headquarters and told the full story. They suggested that the chief get in touch with United States Authorities regarding Caputti and the suspect, who evidently acted as a bodyguard for Benny the Slippery One. The officer thanked them for the information and promised to look into the matter.

When the Drews and the Mises reached home late next afternoon, they found Haruka, the delightful maid whom the family employed, had arranged a special dinner. The reason was that it was Mrs. Mise's birthday!

Haruka had made paper bird and flower decorations using the famous Oregami method. She had hung them in various parts of the dining room. On the table she had put live flowers of various colors interspersed with green vines. In one corner of the room, the maid had placed a huge jardiniere and filled it with lavender wisteria that gently drooped over the sides.

Haruka served a delicious dinner that included strips of fish with rice and fried vegetables. Warm sake, a wine made from rice, was served with the meal. Dessert consisted of a flat piece of plain cake in which the center was scooped out and had been replaced with half of a large, ripe peach. Over it she had poured a hot, pink peach sauce, and she had decorated around the edge with scattered peach leaves.

Everyone enjoyed the delicious meal, and they each proposed toasts to wish Mrs. Mise a happy birthday. When dinner was over, Haruka brought in a large cage with hundreds of gorgeous butterflies in it. She announced that this was her personal gift to Mrs. Mise. She had recently been on vacation and had collected them herself.

"They are beautiful!" Mrs. Mise told her, then translated for the Drews.

"You know my love for the colors blue and yellow," she continued. "How exquisite these butterflies are."

Everyone stood up to look at the fluttering creatures. Nancy liked a particular one that had various shades of blue from light to dark from its center to the wing tips. Mr. Drew's favorite was a reddish brown butterfly with black spots on its wings.

After the excitement about the gift had subsided, Mr. Mise gave his wife his *presento*. It was a high comb studded with pearls for his wife's hair.

"How beautiful!" Nancy exclaimed.

"My husband is a most kind man," Mrs. Mise said. "This is a lovely way to remind me of this birthday."

Nancy and her father were sorry they had not known about the special occasion and did not have a gift for their hostess.

Suddenly Nancy laughed. "Dad," she said, "we brought *presentos* for the Mises from the United States. In all the excitement about villains we completely forgot!" She asked to be excused, went upstairs, and got the gifts from her suitcase. She brought them down and handed a package to each of their friends.

Mr. Mise's *presento* was a new type of fountain pen. After thanking the Drews, he said that he was delighted to own one of them, since they had not yet reached the Japanese market.

His wife's gift was a dainty lace handkerchief. It had been made by a nun who was an expert at needlecraft. She had learned the art in Belgium. Mrs. Mise was thrilled with the *presento*.

Further conversation was interrupted by the ringing of the telephone. Haruka answered and said that it was for Mr. Drew and Miss Nancy. When Mr. Drew said hello, there was a click on the line, and it went dead.

Nancy and her father looked at each other. Was this a hoax, or was Mr. Caputti trying to find out whether the Drews had returned to the Mises' home?

The lawyer asked Haruka if she had any idea from where the call had come.

"It was from overseas, sir," she said. "I am so sorry you were interrupted."

A few minutes went by and the phone rang again. This time Mr. Drew answered it himself.

"Is this the Mise home?" a man asked.

"Yes."

"Am I speaking with Mr. Drew?"

"Yes."

"This is Professor Joji Mise in River Heights," the caller identified himself.

"I'm glad to hear from you," Mr. Drew said. "Did you just call a few minutes ago and were interrupted?"

"Yes. I had to try again. Unfortunately, I have bad news for you."

Nancy, who stood close enough to the receiver to overhear the conversation, felt a chill going down her spine. Instantly she thought of Mr. Moto and Mr. Kikichi.

"I have just learned," the professor went on, "that burglars broke into Mr. Moto's shop. Chief McGinnis asked me to tell you about it. They took everything in the place."

"That is, indeed, bad news," Mr. Drew remarked. "What about Mr. Kikichi?"

"He was beaten unconscious and taken to the hospital. But he is all right now."

"Are there any clues to the burglars?" Mr. Drew inquired.

"Yes, the police think that Benny Caputti and his wife were responsible. Further investigation revealed that they might have fled to Japan. We thought you should know this."

Mr. Drew told the professor of their trip to Nara. "My daughter believes she spotted Mr. Caputti but was stopped from pursuing him by a fake guard." He gave the details of the event, and the professor suggested that the Drews try to locate the couple.

"We'll do our best," Mr. Drew promised. "I suppose the River Heights police are working on this, but we may find some good leads here."

"Fine. I will report this to the chief. And now I would like to say hello to my brother and his wife."

As Mr. Drew said good-by to the professor and handed the phone to Mr. Mise, Nancy felt frustrated. Not only had they failed to find Mr. Moto, but now all his property had been stolen! While she and her father discussed the case, she did not know that a good lead would turn up soon. The Mises joined them a few minutes later, but their conversation was interrupted again when the phone rang a third time.

The call was for Nancy. It proved to be from the chief of the Tokyo police force. "We are holding a woman here who has been using a phony passport," the officer told her. "She resembles the description you gave us of a suspect the other day. Is it possible for you to come here to identify her?"

CHAPTER IX

Identification

WHEN Nancy arrived at Tokyo police headquarters with her father and Mr. Mise, she was taken at once to a brightly lighted room. In the center of it stood a tall, three-sectioned Japanese screen. The young sleuth was told to sit down in a comfortable chair behind it.

To her amazement, she found that she could look through the screen but was not visible to anyone on the other side.

The chief explained that this was a rather recent invention. "Similar screens are being installed in many homes, where it is desirable for the owner to be able to look outside but not to be observed by curious passersby.

He told the young sleuth that presently a woman would walk across the room. Nancy was to observe her carefully and decide if she could identify her.

"She will not give us her name or tell us where she is from," the officer explained. "But she matched the description of the woman you gave us the other day in connection with Mrs. Rossmeyer, so we thought you might be able to help us."

He left the room and she waited eagerly for the suspect to appear. In a few minutes, the door opened again. A woman came in, looking around for anyone watching her. Seeing no one, she walked toward a door on the other side. Nancy had no doubt in her mind that she was indeed Rosina Caputti!

The young detective had a wild desire to dash from behind the screen, confront Rosina, and try to get a confession from her. She wanted to ask questions about Mr. Moto and World Wide Gems. However, she knew that this would be hopeless. Mrs. Caputti would deny everything and refuse to talk.

The woman reached the far side of the room and was about to go out the door, when she apparently changed her mind. With an evil glint in her eyes, she made a beeline for the screen behind which Nancy was sitting. The young sleuth wondered what to do. Should she play a cat and mouse game and dodge to the front of the screen? She had only a fraction of a second to decide. Having identified Mrs. Caputti, she decided to stand her ground.

The next instant, the suspect hurried around to the back. She stopped short and stared at Nancy balefully.

"You little vixen!" she shouted, grabbing the girl by her hair.

Nancy wrenched the woman's hands away and exclaimed, "Leave me alone! It won't do you any good to harm me. You're Rosina Caputti, and you're likely to stay in prison!"

The commotion brought the chief back into the room. "What is going on?" he shouted.

Mrs. Caputti said, "This little busybody was spying on me. I won't have it! Why did you tell me to walk across this room?"

Nancy answered the question. "So I would be able to identify you."

At this Mrs. Caputti screamed and tried to get her hands on the girl again. "I never saw you in my life!"

Nancy, who was athletic and strong, pinned the woman's hands behind her, while the chief called out in Japanese, apparently for help. Another officer appeared instantly. The two men wrestled with Mrs. Caputti, who was fighting them like a tigress. Finally she was hustled away, and the chief returned to Nancy.

"The woman is definitely Rosina Caputti," the girl told him.

"Thank you very much," he said, bowing. "I

"You little vixen!" the woman shouted at Nancy.

did not know she would act like this, but I am glad you were able to identify her."

He and Nancy walked into his office, where Mr. Drew and Mr. Mise were waiting.

Nancy's father asked, "What was all that screaming about?"

The young detective gave him the details, then smiled. "I'm glad the chief rescued me. Mrs. Caputti is much larger than I. I'm not sure I would have won the battle!"

The officer grinned. "I would say you are very strong and agile yourself."

Nancy and her father thanked the chief and said good-by. He replied, *"Sayonara."*

When the three reached home, they found Mrs. Mise upset. Nancy sensed this at once and asked, "While we were gone, did something unpleasant happen?"

Mrs. Mise nodded and replied, "A man, who would not give his name, phoned several times asking for Mr. Drew and Nancy Drew."

"What did you tell him?"

Mrs. Mise smiled. "I said that no one by that name was here. And you were not. You were at the police station."

Her husband said that was very clever, and she went on, "The man made threatening remarks, but would not say who he was. Finally he became angry and said, 'I will not phone again, but tell Mr. Drew and that daughter of his that four plus nine still equals thirteen!' "

"It sounds as if he is getting desperate," Mr. Drew commented.

"And scared," Nancy added. "Maybe this unknown speaker planned to steal the thirteenth pearl, but somebody else got there first. He thinks we know who it was and is trying to find out."

Mr. Drew thought this was a shrewd guess. "Perhaps he's one of the underworld characters, but is being double-crossed by another member."

Nancy knew Mrs. Mise was convinced that she and her father were in grave danger, but their hostess did not express her thoughts aloud. Instead, she said, "I think this evening we should forget all about this mystery and have a good time. If my husband wishes to do so, I suggest that we all go to the Kabuki Theater."

Nancy and her father were delighted with this idea. They had an early supper, then drove to the huge theater. When they took their seats, the Drews were amazed that many people were eating or walking down the aisles, even though the first play had already begun. To Nancy this seemed very rude.

Mr. Mise read her thoughts. "These plays are very old," he said, "and from childhood on people get to know them. Many Japanese can recite them almost line for line, so by eating or walking around, they really do not miss any part of the play with its exquisite poetic lines."

"Why are men in women's parts?" Nancy inquired.

"This goes back to the seventeenth century when the government forbade female actors and dancers on stage. The men, as you can see, are heavily made-up and whitened to resemble women."

"And they speak in falsetto voices," Nancy added, then turned her attention to the play again.

She noticed that when a husband and wife returned to their home, the man walked up to the door, took his sandals off with the toes heading toward the door, and walked in. His wife paused, turned around, and removed her shoes, leaving them pointing outward.

Nancy did not mention this until they were on their way home. Then she asked what it meant.

Mrs. Mise told her that in ancient Japanese custom, the man was the sole owner of his house. Everyone else was a guest, even his wife. For this reason, she had to point her sandals outward, which was the proper position to leave.

The Drews' evening had been most enjoyable. Before going to bed, Mrs. Mise offered their American friends tea. She appeared a few minutes later with a large tray. On it were the necessary utensils: a pot of steaming hot water, pottery tea bowls, a tea container, and a bamboo whisk and dipper. There was also a plate of delicious little bean and sugar cakes.

"Tea was brought to Japan from China in the eighth century," explained Mrs. Mise while she spooned the green powder into the bowls. "It was found to have consoling, calming, and soothing powers, and the masters of the Zen religion made a ritual out of its drinking."

She spooned in just enough water to cover the bottom of the bowls. Then she whirled the wisk between her hands to make the mixture frothy before handing the bowls to the Drews.

"This is the manner in which tea is prepared during the tea ceremony," Mrs. Mise went on. "Everyone sits on the floor on the backs of his heels, with toes crossed and knees together, and all bow low each time before eating or drinking. The hostess has carefully learned the skills of the ceremony in the form sanctified by a great tea master, and her movements are very precise."

They drank the thick, opaque liquid.

"This is good," Nancy said, "but it is slightly bitter."

Mrs. Mise smiled. "The tea ceremony involves deep, true friendship. It is said that love of all humanity is in the tea, not in coffee or any other drink, only in Japanese green tea."

"It is also guaranteed to help you sleep, in case you have any trouble," Mr. Mise added.

But Nancy had no problem falling asleep. She had had a full and exciting day. She did not know how long she had been in bed when she heard her name called softly.

At first the girl was too sleepy to pay attention, but after "Nancy, Nancy, Nancy!" was repeated several times, she became wide awake.

"Who are you?" she asked.

There was no answer to her question, but the speaker demanded, "Have the prisoner released from jail and go home!"

CHAPTER X

Night Scare

WITH the threat ringing in her ears, Nancy jumped out of bed. The voice had come from outside, so she ran to the window and was just in time to see a man reaching the bottom of a tree. Evidently he had climbed it in order to call into Nancy's room.

She ordered him to stop, but knew it was useless. Quickly she grabbed her flashlight and pointed it toward the intruder. By now he was rushing toward some bushes. The light revealed that he was short, had thick, shiny black hair and wore a gray suit!

This was the description Mrs. Rooney had given of the man whom she had seen running from Mr. Moto's store! Could he be Benny Caputti?

Nancy concluded that the incident should be

reported to the police, and that a guard should be posted at the house if the Drews were to remain there.

She put on her robe and slippers and went to her father's room. When he was fully awake, Nancy told him what had happened. He was greatly disturbed, realizing that the man who had climbed the tree might have entered Nancy's room and harmed her!

"I like your idea of a guard," he told his daughter. "In the morning we'll talk it over with the Mises. Actually, I'm embarrassed staying here and putting them through all this trouble. We should offer to move at once."

Mr. Drew went to the telephone and called police headquarters. He reported that a man had been roaming around the Mise property who matched Caputti's description. The officer on duty promised to look out for the suspect.

Nancy finally went back to bed but found it hard to sleep, even though she had closed her window and pulled down the bamboo shade. Finally she dozed off and dreamed about climbing up and down trees after Benny the Slippery One Caputti, but never catching him. She slept later than usual, but no one disturbed the weary detective. When Nancy finally came to breakfast, her father and the Mises were already eating.

Nancy bowed low, which seemed to please her hosts, and said good morning. Mr. Drew had already told the Mises what had happened the evening before. "I mentioned, Nancy, that you and I felt we should leave and not put our kind friends to any more trouble. They wouldn't listen to my proposition. I guess I'm losing my ability to sell an idea."

"That is not the reason!" Mrs. Mise objected. "We are very interested in the case and want to do all we can to help you solve it. That is why we insist you remain here."

Mr. Mise changed the subject by showing the Drews the morning paper. For the benefit of his guests, he had thoughtfully bought an English edition. He pointed to a headline which read:

Daring Robbery in Jewelry Store
Only One Valuable Piece Stolen!

The article said that the theft was most unusual. Although the shop had a burglar alarm system, it had not been set off, and the police were at a loss to explain why. Also, they were puzzled by the fact that the only article taken was a necklace containing 25 pearls. The center pearl was very large and on each side of it were 12 smaller ones.

"That sounds like Mrs. Rossmeyer's!" Nancy exclaimed.

"It does, indeed," Mr. Drew agreed. "What do you think happened?"

"Benny the Slippery One comes to mind," she

replied. "I don't know how he got his nickname, but it could mean that he knows how to turn off burglar alarms and slip in and out of jewelry stores unnoticed."

"You are talking about the same man who climbed the tree last night and called into your room?" Mrs. Mise asked.

"Yes."

"But how could he do two things at the same time?"

"Does the article mention what time the robbery took place, Nancy?" Mr. Drew asked.

"It could have been any time after closing yesterday. When the store's custodian arrived at five-thirty this morning, he discovered that the alarm had been turned off. Thinking this strange, he called the owner of the shop. The man came immediately and discovered that the valuable necklace was missing. He phoned the police and they, in turn, gave the item to the newspaper just before it went to press."

"So Benny had plenty of time for the burglary, either before or after he climbed the tree," Nancy said. "I certainly wish I could find out if that necklace was Mrs. Rossmeyer's."

"Possibly World Wide Gems sold it to that jewelry store," Mr. Drew added, "and then Benny or someone working for him went to get it back."

"To make more money by reselling it!" Mrs. Mise added. "What a racket!"

Just then the telephone rang. Hannah Gruen was calling and said that Mr. Drew should phone his office as soon as it was open. "Meanwhile, I'll talk to Nancy," she added.

The young sleuth was delighted with what Hannah had to tell her. Ned Nickerson, Burt Eddleton, and Dave Evans were coming to River Heights to visit Nancy, George, and Bess. They wanted to know how soon Nancy would be home.

"I told them I thought in about a week," Hannah remarked.

"I'll certainly be there by then," Nancy agreed. "Dad and I hope to wind up the mystery soon." She told Hannah what happened since the Drews had arrived in Japan.

When she came to the part about Caputti climbing the tree and calling into her room, the motherly housekeeper gasped. "Oh, Nancy dear, please watch your step!" she begged.

"Don't worry, Hannah," Nancy replied. "I'm doing my best. This is a very puzzling case."

After good-by's had been said, Nancy wondered what to do next. An idea came to her. She said to her father, "Let's go outdoors and see if we can find any clues to the man who was here last night."

The two excused themselves and walked into the garden. Near the bushes through which the suspect had gone were footprints!

"These are strange," Nancy said. "It's not a

complete impression, just the ball of the foot. We can't deduce much from this, but let's see where the prints lead."

"The fugitive must have been running very fast because only the forward part of the foot is showing," Mr. Drew commented. "He was literally on his toes. Nancy, what can you tell from these prints?"

"That the man is short. He takes short steps but doesn't leap. I'd say he's an excellent runner. This may be another reason for his nickname, Benny the Slippery One, if he, indeed, was the intruder."

The Drews followed the shoe prints until they ended in the street, where it was impossible to trace them any further.

Nancy and her father returned to where they had started their search and examined the area between the bushes and the tree. Here the ground was firmer and no prints were visible. The Drews looked carefully at the bark of the tree, thinking its roughness might have snagged something from the man's clothing.

Soon Nancy detected a few thin, wooly, gray threads. "Dad! These could be from Benny's suit!" she exclaimed.

"You're right," Mr. Drew replied after examining the evidence closely. "I'm sure the police would like to see them."

Carefully Nancy deposited the find in her

pocketbook. "I wonder why he has such a liking for gray suits," she mused, then began to search around the tree.

A few seconds later, the girl sleuth cried out, "Oh, Dad, I've found another good clue!"

CHAPTER XI

A Detective Assists

MR. DREW hurried over to see what Nancy had discovered. She had picked up something from the ground directly under the tree.

"What is it?" he asked.

She held out her hand. In it lay a United States 25-cent piece. "I'm sure that man who climbed the tree dropped this. It implies that he's from our country!"

"You're right," her father agreed.

"Well, we have a fair description of him. He's not very tall, has black hair, wears a gray suit of lightweight wool, and is probably an American. Do you think that's enough for the police to go on?"

"It's a bit sketchy, but it sounds like Benny the Slippery One," her father replied.

When they returned to the house to report their clue, they noticed a man walking up the driveway toward them. They waited for him. He was Japanese but spoke perfect English. He introduced himself as Mr. Natsuke and explained that his name meant *ornamental button*. "My ancestors made them and thus received the family name."

Nancy's eyes twinkled. "If I should forget your name, you won't mind if I call you Mr. Button?"

Mr. Natsuke grinned and said that he was the private detective who had come to watch the Mise house during the daytime. Later he would be relieved by a nightshift man. He carried a radio, over which he could receive messages from headquarters.

Nancy asked him if he could also talk to the chief. "Yes, indeed," Mr. Natsuke replied. "Have you a message for him?"

"Yes, I do," Nancy replied and showed him the American quarter and the shreds of cloth she had discovered in the tree.

"We have already told the chief what the suspect looks like, and I'm sure he would be interested in this bit of evidence from his clothes."

The detective promised to call headquarters at once and take the threads with him when he returned there in the evening.

Nancy and her father thanked him and went

into the house. Mrs. Mise was waiting to give them an invitation. "My husband and I are going to a wedding this afternoon. The parents of the bride have graciously invited you to come. I think you would be interested in watching a Japanese wedding."

The Drews were happy to accept and asked what they should wear.

Mrs. Mise said that she would lend Nancy a pretty kimono and flowers for her hair. Mr. Drew had brought a white summer suit with him, which would be appropriate.

Nancy turned to her father. "We will have to get the bride and groom a *presento,*" she said, and asked if he could go with her to a store where silver pieces were sold.

Mr. Drew nodded, even though Mrs. Mise declared this was not necessary. The Drews insisted, however, so she directed them to a shop within walking distance. Before Nancy and her father left, Mrs. Mise announced that she had a hairdresser's appointment in an hour.

"I believe you would find it interesting to come along," she said to Nancy. "The beauty salon is in the basement of a hotel, and they specialize in getting brides ready for their weddings."

"Perhaps I can get my hair shampooed and set," the girl said. "Then I won't feel that I'm being too inquisitive when I watch a bride prepare."

Mrs. Mise offered to make an appointment for

her and asked the Drews to please be back within an hour.

When Nancy and her father reached the shop, she could not refrain from talking to the manager about the strange jewel theft the night before.

"It was most unfortunate," he commented. "We think we have very tight security, but then, one never knows."

The Drews purchased a filigreed silver basket for the bride. The saleswoman told them such baskets were used by Japanese families to hold tea biscuits and little cakes with fruit. Nancy suggested to her father that they send a bud vase to the bride's parents. Both matters were taken care of, and the saleswoman promised that the gifts would be delivered before the wedding.

Nancy and her father reached home just in time for her to go with Mrs. Mise to the beauty parlor. On the way, the young sleuth kept looking out the rear window. She was sure that a car was following close behind!

"I don't want to frighten you, Mrs. Mise," she said, "but I think the man in back of us might try to harm us. Could you suddenly turn and lose him?"

Mrs. Mise was startled. Then she smiled. "I am not what you call a racing driver, but I think I can get rid of the man."

At the next corner, she made a quick left turn through a yellow light. By the time her pursuer reached the intersection, the signal had changed to red, and traffic prevented him from following. Mrs. Mise made a few more turns to throw off the man completely.

"Good for you!" Nancy said. "You might take up auto racing."

Mrs. Mise smiled merrily. When they reached the hotel in which the hairdresser was located, a uniformed attendant took the car, and Mrs. Mise and Nancy walked into the lobby. They rode an elevator to the beauty salon in the basement. Mrs. Mise announced herself and introduced Nancy. Both were shown to chairs. Nancy noticed that near her a bride was being prepared for her wedding. The young detective marveled at the process.

First, the girl's hair was tied on top of her head in a little knot. She wore a low-cut, sleeveless gown, and the operator rubbed cold cream all over her face, neck, shoulders, back and arms. After a few minutes, the cream was wiped off and white powder was dubbed generously over it with a puff. The same operation was repeated after a little while, and Nancy assumed that the process would continue until the bride-to-be had flesh the color of snow. The American girl was particularly interested in the fact that the back of the bride's neck received special attention.

Mrs. Mise, whose hair had been washed already, reached over and said, "Japanese consider the back of the neck and upper shoulders to be more beautiful than the front of the neck and the chest. That is why it must be pure white."

Nancy nodded. Just then her own attendant arrived and shampooed her hair. Nancy's hair was already combed before the process of whitening the bride was finished.

As the beautician set Nancy's hair in loose pin curls, a dainty batiste slip was pulled cautiously over the bride's head and shoulders. Then she was told to lean back so that her eyebrows could be dyed coal black.

While Nancy was left alone under the dryer, she could give the bride her undivided attention. The operator put pink lipstick on the Japanese girl in three applications. After each one, she brushed it daintily so that the lips finally became like a perfect rosebud. Nancy had to admit that while the girl looked very artificial, she was startlingly beautiful.

After the make-up had been completed, the operator brought in the exquisite bridal kimono and adjusted it properly. At that moment a messenger arrived with a large box containing the wig and hair ornaments. It was gently lifted out and set over the bride's hair.

The headgear was a combination wig and hat that had no crown. A white band went completely around it, and fastened to the band were many combs and pins containing danglers of all sorts.

Once more Mrs. Mise leaned over and explained to Nancy that these were symbols. "They indicate a long, happy life, lovely children, and enough money to be comfortable. The white cloth is called a *tsuno-hakushi*. Translated, that means a horn-concealer. It serves as insurance to the future husband that his bride will try not to show any horns of jealousy."

Nancy grinned as Mrs. Mise got back under her dryer. It was not until both had their hair combed out that they felt free to talk.

Suddenly Mrs. Mise said, "Nancy, didn't you mention a Mrs. Rossmeyer from your country who might be in Japan?"

"Yes. Why?"

Mrs. Mise replied, "I just overheard the girl at the desk say that Mrs. Rossmeyer had called to cancel her appointment."

The information excited Nancy. "Mrs. Mise, please ask the girl if Mrs. Rossmeyer is staying at this hotel."

The Japanese woman smiled and went to the desk. When she returned, her answer was, "Yes, Mrs. Rossmeyer is staying here."

"I must see her at once!" Nancy exclaimed.

"I will wait here while you hurry upstairs and speak to the room clerk." Mrs. Mise said. "Find out which room the woman is staying in."

Nancy nodded and went up the steps to the

lobby. After a short wait, she was able to get the clerk's attention.

"I would like to call on Mrs. Rossmeyer," Nancy said.

CHAPTER XII

Suspicious Taxi Driver

"I'M SORRY, miss, but Mrs. Rossmeyer checked out a few minutes ago," the clerk said.

"Did she say where she was going?" Nancy asked.

He shook his head. "Is it important that you find out?"

"Yes, it is. Very important. Is there any way I can get this information?"

The obliging clerk asked his assistant to take over, then came from behind the desk. With Nancy at his side, he inquired at the travel agency in the hotel and asked several porters and the maid who took care of Mrs. Rossmeyer's room.

His efforts were in vain, until a porter, just coming in from outside, told him that the socialite had departed for the airport.

Nancy thanked the kind clerk, then telephoned the Mise home. The maid answered and said that both Mr. Drew and Mr. Mise had gone into the city on business.

"Then may I speak to the man who is guarding the house?" Nancy asked.

When Mr. Natuske came to the phone, she told him what she had learned about Mrs. Rossmeyer's departure.

"Do you know where Mr. Mise has gone?" Nancy asked him.

"Yes, to his bank."

Nancy requested its name, then made a call. She was able to catch Mr. Mise and told him about Mrs. Rossmeyer. "Could you get in touch with the airport authorities and find out where she's going?"

Mr. Mise promised to do so at once.

Nancy returned to the beauty salon. She and Mrs. Mise paid their bills, then left the hotel. On the way home, Nancy told her companion what she had learned from the clerk, and that Mr. Mise would follow the trail.

When they arrived at the house, Nancy went to talk further with Mr. Natsuke. She asked him if anything had happened since she had spoken to him on the phone.

"Yes," he replied. "I saw a man sneaking around the house and taking pictures of both the first and second floors. Unfortunately, I could not get to him in time. He spotted me and ran like a deer."

"What did he look like?" Nancy asked.

"He was Japanese, of medium height, and wore a dark business suit. I got in touch with headquarters and reported it."

Nancy remarked that the people who had been spying on the Mise property now obviously realized that it was being guarded. "I hope none of them will return!"

Mr. Natsuke agreed whole-heartedly.

Nancy had just entered the house when Mr. Mise returned. Eagerly she asked him if he had any luck chasing Mrs. Rossmeyer.

"Yes and no," the Japanese replied. "I was told by the airline that she and her maid departed for Rome. But just before leaving, there had been a commotion in the terminal building."

"A commotion?" Nancy asked in surprise.

Mr. Mise nodded. "When the police rushed up, they learned that Mrs. Rossmeyer had been robbed of two strands of pearls and a valuable ruby and pearl pin!"

"How dreadful!" Nancy exclaimed, then asked if the authorities had obtained any clues to the thieves.

"Perhaps," Mr. Mise replied. "Mrs. Rossmeyer said she suspected the driver of a private taxi that had picked her up at the hotel. She had used him several times before while in Japan and had always found him honest. But now he is a prime suspect because he was the only person near her during the trip to the airport. He took her bags and assisted her from the cab. The theft could have happened then."

"Did the police get his name and address?" Nancy asked.

Mr. Mise said Mrs. Rossmeyer had given it to them. "He is Joe Slate, a Japanese, although he was born in the United States. He drives Americans who speak only English."

"Did the authorities get in touch with him?"

"They called his home, and there was no answer. When they went to his house, they found that he had disappeared. He lived in a furnished apartment, and all his belongings were gone."

Nancy wondered if he could be a member of the Caputti gang, since it specialized in jewel robberies. She asked Mr. Mise if immigration and customs officials had been consulted.

"I do not know, but I will contact both of them," he said.

Mr. Mise spent some time on the telephone. When he returned to Nancy, he said, "Neither immigration nor customs has any record of a Joe Slate."

Nancy wondered if any fellow cabbies might have some information on him and suggested that Mr. Mise speak to the police again and ask for an inquiry of all taxi drivers in Toyko, public or private.

An hour later came a preliminary report. No one who had been questioned so far had any idea where Joe Slate had gone.

"He slipped through our fingers," Nancy said, disappointed.

"Well, there are still a few drivers who have not been questioned yet. And a policeman is stationed across the street from Slate's apartment in case he should come back. If a clue should turn up, the police will call us."

Just then Mr. Drew arrived. He had visited another client, then called on a Tokyo lawyer who was an acquaintance of his. "I did some sleuthing of my own," he said, "and asked this man about Rosina Caputti."

"Oh, good!" Nancy said. "What did he tell you?"

"She's still in jail because the passport she was using had been stolen from a woman she resembles. Fortunately, it's now in the possession of its owner. But Mrs. Caputti still refuses to tell why she was using a false passport to enter the country."

"That's no news," Nancy said.

"The news is coming now," Mr. Drew said with a smile. "Mrs. Caputti had a caller in jail. He gave his name as Joe Slate."

"Joe Slate!" Nancy exclaimed. "That's the

name of Mrs. Rossmeyer's private taxi driver who is suspected of having robbed her!"

She told her father the story and asked if he had obtained a description of Joe Slate.

"He's Japanese, medium height, and speaks English without an accent," Mr. Drew replied.

"He sounds like the same man who drove Mrs. Rossmeyer!" Nancy declared.

Mr. Drew frowned. "This is very puzzling. You say Slate has disappeared? He had told Mrs. Caputti that he would get a lawyer for her. So far no one has come."

"How long ago did he visit her?"

"I believe just yesterday."

At this moment Mrs. Mise walked up to them. "I do not mean to interrupt," she said politely, "but we must dress for the reception if we do not wish to be late."

Nancy and her father excused themselves and went off to change their clothes. When they appeared a little while later, Mr. Drew declared that he had never seen his daughter look prettier.

Nancy's eyes twinkled. "You mean I might have made a good Japanese girl?"

He grinned back at her. "You certainly would have made a good Japanese detective!"

Mr. and Mrs. Mise looked charming in their outfits, but Nancy could not help but think how distinguished her father looked in his white, formal dress.

"The ceremony will be attended only by close

members of the family," Mrs. Mise told Nancy on the way to the hotel where the reception was to be held.

"I'm sorry," Nancy said. "I would have loved to have seen it."

"I can tell you a little about the ceremony," Mrs. Mise said. "Most weddings take place, as we Japanese say, 'before the Shinto Gods.' Sometimes this is only a scroll with the name of a God hanging in front of the couple as they exchange their vows, but mostly a Shinto priest presides. He must exorcise any evil influences that the couple might be exposed to, and does this with a shake of the streamers attached to a wand."

"And then they drink the ceremonial drink?" Nancy asked. "I've heard about that."

"Yes. That is the most important part of the ceremony. Both bride and groom must take the ritual drink, three times, then another three times, then another—nine times in all. After this the bride removes her headgear, signifying that she has left her family. There are no rings or other tokens exchanged at a Japanese wedding."

"I heard that in the olden days the groom was not allowed to see the bride's face until after the wedding," Nancy spoke up.

"That is true. It was feared that if he saw it, he might not wish to marry her. The removal of the hat is still the symbolic gesture of showing her face."

When they reached the reception, they found the newlyweds seated at the head of a long table, while the bride's and groom's families were on opposite sides.

"You see the elderly man next to the couple?" Mrs. Mise said to Nancy. "He is the sponsor of the wedding. In this case, he is a senior member of the accounting firm for whom the groom works."

Just then the man stood up and spoke in Japanese. "He's presenting the couple to the party," Mrs. Mise explained. "He tells about their families and their achievements."

After the speech, various guests sang short songs, some of which, Mrs. Mise said, were from plays.

As the festivities proceeded, guests mingled and spoke to the young couple and their parents. Nancy noticed the many jewels the women were wearing. There were not only pearls in abundance, but diamonds, rubies, sapphires, emeralds, and semiprecious stones. All of them were gorgeous. Most of the women wore fancy head-combs.

Nancy thought, "What a wonderful place for a thief like Benny the Slippery One to operate!"

After wishing the bride and groom great happiness in their married life and thanking the newlyweds' parents for inviting them, the Drews followed the Mises toward a table with dainty refreshments.

They had been there only a few minutes when

one of the hotel's messenger boys walked up to Mr. Mise. He handed him a letter and spoke in Japanese.

After he left, Mr. Mise opened the envelope. Inside was another one addressed to Nancy. A bit nervous about what its contents might be, she took out the message. It read:

$4 + 9 = 13$. *Your time is getting short!*

CHAPTER XIII

The Party Thief

MRS. MISE was very upset, and she was on the verge of tears. "This is so bad," she said, "so very bad."

Nancy patted the woman's hands. "Let's try not to take this warning too seriously. I think that whoever has been writing these notes is a coward. If not, he would have done something more drastic by this time."

Mr. Drew knew that Nancy was trying to make their hostess feel better. He doubted, however, that Nancy could take the matter so lightly.

He was right. Secretly Nancy was greatly worried. She had a feeling that her adversary desperately wanted to frighten her. Nancy asked Mr. Mise if he would try to find the porter who had brought him the note. "I'll go with you," she added.

Together they hurried to the lobby of the hotel and walked past the porters who were seated on a bench in a little niche.

Mr. Mise shook his head. "I don't see the young man here," he declared. "Maybe he was from another hotel."

Nancy asked, "Did he wear the same uniform as these men?"

Mr. Mise nodded. "That means he could not be from another hotel." Suddenly a smile crossed his face. "Here he comes now!"

A young man was walking out of an elevator. Mr. Mise and Nancy went up to him, and the two Japanese conversed for a few minutes. Then Mr. Mise translated for Nancy.

"The porter says that a little boy arrived with the note, then left the hotel. He does not know whether the child came from the street or whether he is staying at the hotel."

"In other words, someone probably gave him a tip to bring the note to the porter, so the real sender couldn't be traced," Nancy reasoned. "Very clever."

"Whom do you suspect the sender is?" Mr. Mise asked.

"Benny Caputti. He either followed us or happened to see us here. If the latter is true, he was in the hotel. In either case, he might still be here!"

"And you would like to find him," Mr. Mise said with a smile. "But it is a large place, and you cannot search the rooms!"

"I know," Nancy said. "But Benny would be where the jewelry is—"

"Which is at the reception!" Mr. Mise completed her sentence.

"Right. Let's go back there and tell Dad."

When Mr. Drew and Mrs. Mise heard about what had happened, they offered to look around for a man who matched Caputti's description. Nancy and her father went off together. The Mises walked in a different direction.

Presently Nancy noticed a short, black-haired man who, although he was not dressed in a gray suit, was obviously American or European like Caputti. He was walking quietly among the guests, when Mr. Mise appeared on the scene and took her arm.

"Nancy, I would like you to meet Mr. Shopwell. He is president of an American bank in Tokyo."

Nancy managed to hide her surprise and shook hands with Mr. Shopwell. How glad she was that she had said nothing!

The Drews and Mr. Mise spoke to the bank president for a while, then continued their sleuthing. Nancy saw another man some distance away who was dressed in black dinner clothes and fit the description of Benny the Slippery One. Suddenly she stopped short and grabbed her father's arm.

"Look!" she said. "That man! He's snipping a pearl necklace right off that woman's neck!"

The young detective and her father made their way through the crowd to close in on the thief, who had slipped the necklace into his right pants pocket.

He was walking away from the woman with quick steps. When Nancy and her father caught up to him, they each took an arm.

"We saw you steal that woman's necklace!" Nancy accused him.

"That is a lie!" the thief cried out.

"You can't deny it," Mr. Drew said. "The necklace is in your right pants pocket!"

The suspect stepped a few paces away. "You are wrong!" he insisted, still backing up further. "You are wrong. I'll prove it to you!" With that he turned the pocket inside out.

Several coins fell to the floor, but that was all. The pearl necklace was not among them!

Nancy and her father were stunned. It seemed like the work of a magician. The Drews had to agree that the necklace was indeed not there and apologized as the man angrily pushed the pocket back into its place. Then he picked up his coins from the floor.

"But I saw you take it!" Nancy insisted. "I'm

"He's slipping a pearl necklace off that woman's neck!"
Nancy said.

sure I saw you take it. But if I was wrong, I'm sorry."

The man nodded and turned to leave. The Drews walked away quickly before there might be a scene.

"I can't understand what happened," Mr. Drew said tensely. "We both watched him take that necklace!"

"I have an idea," Nancy spoke up. "Maybe there was a hole in his pocket, the pearls fell to the floor, and were picked up by an accomplice! Remember, there were a few people between us and that man, so we might not have seen the necklace drop."

"You're right," her father agreed. "Let's go back to the spot and see what we can learn."

By the time they reached the area where the theft had occurred, the owner had discovered her loss. She was Japanese, and began exclaiming in bitter tones in her language. The Drews did not understand what she was saying but noticed another guest hurrying up to her. She was an American who apparently understood some Japanese. However, she spoke to the woman in English. "I saw a necklace on the floor a few minutes ago. A Japanese woman picked it up, slipped it into her purse, and walked off. I assumed it belonged to her."

Mr. Drew whispered to his daughter, "You were right about the hole in the thief's pocket.

'And the woman who picked up the necklace was indeed an accomplice."

Nancy was annoyed at herself for letting the thief slip through her fingers so easily. Why had she not looked for a hole in his pocket when he turned it inside out?

She spoke to the guest who had watched the person pick up the pearls from the floor. "Would you recognize her if you saw her again?"

"I believe I would," the American replied. "She wore a very pretty kimono and carried a matching handbag."

"Would you mind pointing her out to me?"

When the woman hesitated, Nancy added, "I'm trying to catch a thief, and I believe he's at this party."

The American consented, while Mr. Drew asked other guests if any of their jewelry was missing. Suddenly there was a hubbub as one woman after another discovered that their gems had been stolen. Bracelets, necklaces, pins, and hair ornaments were gone. A valuable ruby and diamond necklace was reported by a friend of the bride to have been stolen.

Mr. Mise notified the police, and a number of officers arrived in a few minutes to search for the thief. All guests cooperated and permitted themselves to be searched.

A young officer asked Nancy for her purse. She smiled.

"I don't have one with me," she said. "I put my comb into the bottom of my kimono sleeve as I understand Japanese women often do."

"Then I must examine your sleeves," the officer said.

He found nothing in the left one, then reached into the right. To Nancy's horror he pulled out a gorgeous ruby and diamond necklace!

CHAPTER XIV

The Trap

NANCY was so shocked at seeing the beautiful necklace taken from her sleeve that for a moment she was speechless.

Her father came to her defense. "This is ridiculous. My daughter certainly does not own that and did not take it from anyone."

The officer asked how she could explain its presence in her sleeve. "You had better come up with a good story, or I will have to take you to headquarters!" he said sternly.

"I have already spoken to the chief about a case I'm working on involving stolen jewelry," Nancy said.

The officer raised his eyebrows in amazement.

"It started in the United States," the girl detective went on. "A valuable necklace was stolen from a jeweler in my hometown just before the jeweler mysteriously disappeared. My father and

I came here to investigate because several leads pointed to Japan. We hope to locate the stolen piece and also the thief."

"Is it *this* necklace?" the officer asked.

"No. But I saw a very suspicious man take a string of pearls from a woman. When I accused him, he denied it. Since he didn't have it on his person, we couldn't prove it, and he left. Then other people complained about having their jewelry stolen. I know he framed me before slipping out so I could not pursue him any longer!"

Nancy gave more details of the case, and the young officer did not know how to proceed. Since evidence was found on her person, could he legally let her go?

By this time Mr. and Mrs. Mise had come up to Nancy and her father and asked what the trouble was. They knew the officer. As soon as they heard what had happened, both vouched for Nancy, saying the accusation was unjust.

The policeman finally agreed to release Nancy into the Mises' custody if they would guarantee her appearance in court if she were called. Mr. Mise promised.

The commotion over the jewelry thefts had ruined the wedding reception. Nancy and her father went to find the bride and groom and their parents, but all of them had left.

"I certainly feel sorry for them," Nancy declared. "It should have been such a happy occasion. To have something like this happen will be an unfortunate memory for them."

Mr. Drew and the Mises agreed.

"I see they have opened the doors once more," Mr. Mise said. "I suppose they did not find the thief and his accomplice. Evidently they escaped before the doors were closed. We may as well go home ourselves now."

He kept in close touch with the police for the next few hours, but learned nothing helpful. Had the reception thieves left the country, or was Caputti still in Japan?

Mrs. Mise remarked, "As long as Mrs. Caputti is in jail, I doubt that her husband would leave town."

"He might," Mr. Drew said. "Benny's a very cruel man."

The following morning Nancy asked Mr. Mise if he would take her and her father back to the World Wide Gems offices to talk to Mr. Kampura about the case. He was not in, and the only person available was Mr. Hashi, the local manager.

When questioned by the Drews about the various jewel thefts, he said he knew nothing about them. Nancy asked him if he was aware that World Wide Gems was under suspicion.

"Oh, no! We are a reputable organization!" he replied. "Where did you hear such a rumor?"

Nancy gave no details but thought she detected a frown on the man's face. Other than that, he showed no sign of being disturbed. Instead, he insisted on the fine reputation of the company and that it was considered the finest jewelry wholesaler in the world.

"That must be of great satisfaction to you and the other executives," Nancy said. "Actually we were told that the president and other top officials are not directly involved."

Mr. Hashi was annoyed. He took this remark as an inference that *he* might be under suspicion, not being a top official himself.

"If you are implying that I am dishonest, I wish to inform you that my integrity has never been questioned. Now I must say good-by to you," he said coldly.

He arose, then bowed stiffly and held this position until the callers had left his office. As they were walking down the hallway, the visitors came face to face with Mr. Taro, the president of the company. He wished them a pleasant morning and kept on going.

Nancy stopped him. "Mr. Taro," she said, "we came to ask if any jewelry has been offered to you by a Mr. Caputti or a Mr. Slate."

"No, neither one of them has been here," the man replied. "In fact, recently no one has come to me with anything valuable to sell."

"Thank you," Nancy said, and her group continued toward the elevator.

Suddenly her father turned around and hurried back to Mr. Taro. "Pardon me," he said to the president, "but it is important for me as a lawyer to know whether you, as head of this company, are aware of the fact that World Wide Gems is presently under suspicion of underhanded dealings."

Mr. Taro laughed. "It is impossible. You heard a rumor that is absolutely not true." With that, he hurried on.

Mr. Drew joined Nancy and Mr. Mise in front of the elevator. Before it arrived, a young Japanese woman, who evidently worked for World Wide Gems, approached them.

"Follow me," she said to Nancy in a low voice. "I can tell you something important!"

Nancy signaled to her father to watch where they were going in case of foul play, then walked quickly after the woman to a ladies restroom.

When the door was closed behind them, the stranger said, "I cannot stay away from my desk very long or my boss will be suspicious. I am Mr. Taro's secretary, and I am worried about him. He is an honest man, but recently he has become suspicious of certain officials in the company. He is afraid that they are carrying on some dishonest schemes in regard to the purchase of jewelry."

Nancy nodded. "He probably didn't want to admit it to us. How did you find out about it?"

"I overheard a conversation on his private telephone line. I do not know to whom he was speaking, but the other person said, "Yes, I received a warning note that said four plus nine equals thirteen."

Nancy was startled. The look on her face prompted the young woman to ask whether she knew what it meant.

"I have an idea it stands for danger," Nancy replied, but did not mention having received several similar warnings.

"I know you are a detective," the Japanese woman went on. "I spent some time in your country and read about you. When I overheard your name today, I felt I could trust you. I am so worried about Mr. Taro. Perhaps you can help him. He is a wonderful person, and I do not wish to have any harm come to him."

"I'm glad you told me," Nancy said. "I'll do my best."

"Thank you," the girl said. "Now I must go."

She opened the door and hurried out quickly. Nancy waited several seconds before following her, so that no one in the hallway would suspect that they had been talking. Then she joined her father and Mr. Mise again. They all went down and walked into the street.

When they arrived home Nancy told her story so that Mrs. Mise could hear it, too. When she was finished, everyone was shocked.

"This is a most complicated affair," Mrs. Mise said. "Those jewel thieves are dreadful people!"

"I have a feeling that top officials at World Wide Gems who are not involved with the underworld might be in grave danger. They must have found out certain things and are now being threatened."

"And the criminals would stop at nothing to gain their ends," Mr. Mise added. "I am so worried about both of you."

The Drews did not feel comfortable either, but said that they had been in precarious situations before and never quit when they were hot on the trail of wrongdoers.

"I'd like very much to see a list of all people working for World Wide Gems," she added.

Mr. Mise jumped up from his chair. "It just occurred to me that I have one. I own a small amount of stock in the company. A list came with the annual report. However, it gives only the names of officers."

"That's enough to start with," Nancy said, and he went to get it. Nancy and her father read the names of the many vice presidents.

Suddenly the girl exclaimed, "Look! I can't believe it!"

"Don't tell me Mr. Caputti is an executive of World Wide Gems," her father teased.

"No, but wait until you hear who is! *Mrs. Tanya Rossmeyer!*"

Mr. Drew stared at her. "You're kidding!" I had no idea that she was active in any business."

"She certainly doesn't act like a business woman," Nancy added, "traveling from one place to another without telling anyone her schedule."

"That's true," her father agreed. "On the other hand, with her love and knowledge of gems, she would be qualified."

"She had some quite valuable jewelry stolen," Nancy mused. "Perhaps she was allowing herself to be robbed by a confederate of the company as a cover up! Dad, Mrs. Rossmeyer could be in league with the thieves at World Wide Gems!"

Mrs. Mise had sat down in one corner and started to read the morning paper. Suddenly she cried out, "Here is an amazing article!"

"What does it say?" Nancy asked.

"It is a report from Rome that states that Mrs. Tanya Rossmeyer, while attending a dinner, was robbed of a priceless necklace!"

CHAPTER XV

Phony Papers

"WHAT else does the newspaper article say?" Nancy asked Mrs. Mise.

The Japanese woman continued to read, then translated. "The police have been unable to locate Mrs. Rossmeyer since the theft. Newsmen and friends have not heard from her either."

Mrs. Mise went on reading. "It was conjectured that Mrs. Rossmeyer might have left for the United States. Police and friends have said that oftentimes, on a whim, she would pack up, leave wherever she was, and not tell anyone where she was going. Then suddenly she would turn up in a different country."

"She might have gone home to River Heights," Nancy speculated. "One thing we have never asked about is the companion who is said to travel with her. Was she with Mrs. Rossmeyer? Is she mixed up in the jewel racket?"

Mr. Mise spoke up. "Would you like me to call the newspaper and ask if they have any information about the woman?"

"Please do," Nancy replied.

Mr. Mise went to the phone. He returned in a short time to say that when last seen, Mrs. Rossmeyer's companion was with her. "Would you like to go to headquarters and talk to the chief?"

"Yes," Nancy and her father replied together.

The chief had little to add to the newspaper story, but while his visitors waited, he made a long distance call to the chief of police in Rome. Then he reported that an investigation had been made, and anyone who might have any information on the jewel theft or the whereabouts of Mrs. Rossmeyer had been questioned thoroughly.

"One person overheard the two women talking about returning to the United States," he added. "But someone else had heard them mention that they would go to Paris. Where they went, nobody knows."

Nancy asked him what he knew about World Wide Gem's recent business dealings. When Nancy told of her theory regarding Mrs. Rossmeyer, the chief nodded.

"We do not feel that she is involved in any dishonest dealings," he said. "All the information we have collected indicates that Mrs. Rossmeyer is not really active as an officer of World Wide

Gems. It was advantageous for them to use her name, which is synonymous with fine jewelry and good advertising. But we are still investigating all angles."

The telephone rang, and the chief answered. After a brief conversation he hung up and said, "I just had a message from Interpol. Someone in your hometown claims to have seen the missing Mr. Moto in the back seat of an automobile. The police strongly suspect that he never left River Heights!"

Nancy and her father looked at each other. "I had almost come to the same conclusion," she said.

After thanking the chief, they drove back to the Mise home. Mrs. Mise had a message for Mr. Drew. His office had called and indicated that it was important for him to return home as soon as possible.

"In view of what we just heard at headquarters," Mr. Drew said to Nancy, "I don't think it would be worthwhile for you to stay, either. Both Mr. Moto and Mrs. Rossmeyer are obviously not in Japan, and I don't believe you can do any more to locate Mr. Caputti than the police can."

Nancy agreed. She felt it was more important to follow the clue to Mr. Moto, who, she was convinced now, was being held against his will by someone in his hometown. Also, in the back of her mind was the statement from Bess and George that Ned, Burt, and Dave were coming to visit the girls in River Heights.

"Maybe they can help us hunt," she thought.

The Drews told their hosts that they were planning to leave the following day.

"Oh, we must have a farewell party," Mrs. Mise said at once.

"That's very sweet of you," Nancy said, "but it is not necessary. Anyway, we are not giving you enough time to plan anything."

Mrs. Mise said, "Perhaps, as you say, there is not enough time to invite friends, but I suggest that we go to Mr. Mise's club this evening. It has a very fine restaurant, and I think you will enjoy the food there."

The club proved to be not only an excellent place to eat, but it was filled with many interesting art objects. A lovely Japanese girl named Lei greeted them. She wore a beautiful flowered satin kimono with a contrasting obi. She had a very fetching high hair-do accented by combs. Lei showed them several charming old pictures of Japanese life as it was hundreds of years ago.

Mr. Drew was particularly interested in pictures of old-time Japanese fishermen using the cormorant bird to make their catch. They held the bird like a kite on a string. When the cormorant swooped down to the water and scooped up a fish in its bill, the fisherman would quickly pull it in and take the catch!

"The poor cormorant!" Nancy said. "He worked so hard for nothing."

Their guide smiled. "I venture to say that the fishermen allowed the birds to have their fill after they did their job."

Next to the pictures, Lei showed them jeweled crowns, which she said had been worn by royal children in various countries. She pointed to one, which she said was Russian.

"Long ago girls usually married young in that country. The brides were shaved in order to accommodate the crown jewels they would wear," she explained.

While the group was eating, the headwaiter told Mr. Mise that he had read about the disappearance of Mrs. Tanya Rossmeyer.

"She is a member of our club," he remarked. "I hope nothing has happened to her. She was here only a short while ago."

"Did she by any chance mention to you where she was going after her visit to Rome?" Mr. Drew inquired.

"No. I have no idea. She frequently travels from place to place."

When the group arrived home, Nancy and her father packed. They were booked to fly to the United States the following evening.

"It's high time we get back and take up our work," the lawyer said.

"I can hardly wait," Nancy added.

After breakfast, the young detective said she would like to go to the jail and try to talk to Mrs. Caputti.

"Maybe if I tell her I know a lot about the jewel thefts, she may break down and confess," Nancy reasoned.

"I doubt it," her father said, "but I suppose it's worth a try."

Mrs. Mise offered to go along, and when the two arrived, they asked to see the warden. After introducing themselves, they inquired whether it would be possible to speak to Mrs. Caputti.

The warden smiled. "So sorry," he said. "Her lawyer came here with certain papers and she was released."

"Released!" Nancy exclaimed. She was stunned. "But I'm sure there must be some mistake. Mrs. Caputti's husband is wanted in the United States, and we believe she works with him in committing jewel robberies!"

The warden shrugged. "I am certain you must be wrong. I told you, her lawyer came here with the papers."

"What did he look like?" Nancy asked.

"He was tall for a Japanese, and powerfully built. Rather stern faced, I would say."

The truth dawned on the girl detective. "What was his name?"

"Mr. Kampura!"

CHAPTER XVI

Mysterious Invitation

"Oh no!" Nancy exclaimed in dismay.

The warden stared at her. "What is wrong?"

"Mr. Kampura is suspected of dishonest dealings. I'm sure he forged those papers. Will you please check them and verify the signature?"

By now the warden felt uncomfortable. "Of course. I will get them from my file," he said, and left. A few minutes later he returned with a folder. "The documents were signed by Judge Hiawasa. I shall call him at once and confirm his signature."

He phoned the judge's chambers and apparently found him in. After a brief conversation in Japanese, the warden hung up. His face ashen white. "You were right. Judge Hiawasa never issued an order for the release of the woman prisoner. Oh, what have I done!"

"You let a known criminal out of jail," Nancy said. "But it was not your fault," she added, realizing the man's distress. "I'm sure the forgery was an excellent one."

The warden promised to get in touch with higher authorities at once. He thanked Nancy and Mrs. Mise for their help, and both said they were glad to have been of some service to him.

Nevertheless, they were worried about Mrs. Caputti being free and spoke about it on the way home. "I suppose now she'll join her husband," Nancy said, "and perhaps they will leave the country together, if he has not already gone."

When Mrs. Mise and Nancy reached home, the girl detective packed her bags. Then their hosts drove the Drews to the airport and said good-by.

"Be sure to let us know how you progress with the case," Mr. Mise said.

"Indeed we will," Nancy replied. "We never can thank you enough for your help in trying to solve this international case."

In the airport Nancy and her father looked carefully for the Caputtis. There was no sign of them, and finally Nancy and her father boarded their plane.

When they reached River Heights the next day and walked into their own house, Hannah was overjoyed to see them. After she and Nancy exchanged hugs, Mrs. Gruen said she had worried every minute during the Drews' absence.

"Any special reason?" Nancy's father asked her.

The housekeeper said that several phone calls had come for them. When she told the persons that the Drews were not at home, they had left various messages.

"I've written them all down for you to look at later. Some of them were warnings of one sort or another. Several of the callers demanded to know how to get in touch with you. Of course, I did not tell them, and while I didn't say so, my answers inferred that you were only out of town temporarily."

"Good for you!" Mr. Drew praised her. "You probably saved us a lot of trouble."

When Nancy walked into the dining room, she was amazed to see the table set for a number of people.

"Who's coming?" she asked.

Hannah Gruen smiled. "Three guesses."

Nancy counted the number of places, then said, "Bess, George, Ned, Burt, and Dave."

"Correct."

Before the guests arrived, Nancy unpacked her clothes and the gifts she had brought. Hurrying downstairs, she put the boxes at the places where each recipient would sit, and she attached cards.

'All the guests arrived in a little while. Bess said, "Oh, Nancy, I'm so happy you're home safe and sound," and hugged her.

George was eager to hear about Nancy's adventures. "And don't leave out a word!" she commanded.

Burt and Dave, both strong, sturdy football players, greeted the Drews enthusiastically, saying they were envious of their exciting trip. Ned, more handsome than the others, had brown eyes, wavy dark hair, and a ready smile. He gave Nancy an affectionate embrace.

"It's sure great to have you back," he said.

The dinner was filled with fun and excitement, and the guests were thrilled with their presents. Hannah, Bess, and George put on their necklaces, while Ned fastened his stickpin to his necktie. Burt and Dave were surprised to receive anything, but Nancy explained that their gifts were actually from Bess and George, who had given her money to buy souvenirs for their friends.

"They're neat!" all the recipients exclaimed, and Hannah hurried to the mirror to admire her matching necklace and earrings.

"And now tell us about your trip and what sleuthing you did in Japan," George begged.

Nancy and her father kept their audience spellbound for some time. Bess actually shivered at the episode of the man calling into her bedroom at the Mises', and again at the frame-up when the necklace was found in Nancy's kimono sleeve.

"I'm afraid we didn't accomplish as much as we had hoped," the young sleuth said. "We think, however, that we will be able to continue our work from here."

When Nancy finished her account, Mr. Drew turned to Bess and George. "Suppose you tell us what you've been doing during our absence."

George smiled. "We watched Mr. Moto's shop whenever we could to see if Mr. Kikichi would do anything suspicious."

"Did he?" Nancy asked eagerly.

"No. Not a thing. But one day on the way home we saw Mr. Moto in the back seat of a car. At least we think it was Mr. Moto. He seemed to be asleep. Perhaps he was drugged."

"George, that's a wonderful clue!" Nancy exclaimed. "We heard it from the Tokyo police chief but had no idea that it came from you!"

"We reported it to Chief McGinnis," Bess took up the story. "He promised to pass the information on to you."

"We tried to follow the car," George said, "but lost it in traffic."

"Did you get the license number?" Mr. Drew asked.

"Yes," Bess replied. "The police checked it out and found that the car was stolen. It was discovered the following day in a supermarket parking lot."

"Too bad," Nancy said.

As the group at the table was eating dessert, the telephone rang. Nancy, being nearest the hall door, jumped up and answered it.

"Is this Miss Nancy Drew?" a man's voice asked.

"Yes."

"I am a friend of Mr. Moto's. As you know, he's planning to go to Japan. Mrs. Rossmeyer is home now and is giving a surprise farewell party for him. She would like very much to have you come."

"Mr. Moto is still in this country?" Nancy asked, pretending to be surprised.

"Yes. The party will be tomorrow night at her home at eight o'clock. Please bring an escort if you wish. When you arrive, say to the doorman, 'Twelve and thirteen'."

Nancy, frowning, walked back to the table and sat down. "I was just invited to a surprise party and told to bring an escort," she explained to her friends.

"Who called?" Bess inquired.

"A friend of Mr. Moto's!"

"You're kidding!" Ned burst out. "Did he give his name?"

"No. He said the party would be held by Mrs.

Rossmeyer as a send-off for Mr. Moto, who is going to Japan."

"Then Mrs. Rossmeyer is home?" Mr. Drew asked.

"Apparently."

Hannah Gruen shook her head. "This is very strange. Mrs. Rossmeyer plans a party. There are no formal invitations, Mr. Moto appears mysteriously at Mrs. Rossmeyer's, and you're invited. She doesn't even know you! Something's fishy. I don't believe you should go."

"Hannah is probably right," Mr. Drew agreed. "What else did the man say, Nancy?"

"That was it, except he told me to introduce myself and my escort by the numbers twelve and thirteen."

"That does it!" Hannah cried out. "It's a trap! Nancy, I am afraid you are in great danger if you accept!"

"But if I don't, I might miss a wonderful chance to solve the mystery!" Nancy objected. "And if Ned comes with me and we're careful, I'm sure we can avoid falling into any trap. Ned, are you game to go?"

"I wouldn't miss it for the world," he replied. He flexed the muscles in his arms. "Bring on your crooks."

Everybody laughed, then Bess asked, "If Mr. Moto was responsible for losing Mrs. Rossmeyer's valuable necklace with the thirteenth pearl, why should she be giving a farewell party for him?"

Still puzzled, the group sat around the table for a long while. Then Bess and George said they should leave. Burt and Dave went with them. After Nancy had helped Hannah tidy up, the housekeeper and Mr. Drew said they were going to retire.

Nancy and Ned stayed in the living room for some time discussing what they might expect at Mrs. Rossmeyer's party. Nancy smiled. "I suppose I'll have to dress up."

"I brought party clothes myself," Ned announced. "One never knows what a guest of yours may be expected to do, or where he might be asked to go, so I came prepared with all sorts of clothes."

The house was very quiet, with Togo asleep in the kitchen. The couple sat in semidarkness. Not a sound came from outdoors, until suddenly there were footsteps and a commotion near the front door.

Nancy and Ned jumped up to see what it was. Ned took hold of Nancy's arm. "Don't open the door," he warned. "You have been in so much trouble, and this might be more of it."

A man's voice outside shouted, "Open up or we'll break down the door!"

Nancy and Ned did not move. The warning

was not repeated. Instead, there was a splintering crash, and the front door burst open. A huge vicious dog bounded inside, directly at the couple!

CHAPTER XVII

Pounds of Jewelry

BEFORE the police dog could attack Nancy and Ned, they bounded into the living room, jumped over the back of a sofa that stood cater-cornered to the wall, and dropped to the floor.

The furious animal jumped onto the sofa and snarled at them. He did not pounce on the couple, however, apparently afraid of being caught in the narrow enclosure.

"Help! Help!" Nancy and Ned shouted at the top of their lungs.

Suddenly the man at the front door called out, "This is your last warning!"

The big dog, meanwhile, had jumped off the sofa and tried to crawl underneath it in order to get at Nancy and Ned. He succeeded only partway, but kept snarling at the trapped couple.

"Help!" Nancy cried out again. "But be careful! There's a vicious dog in here!"

Just then her father came running down the stairway in his bathrobe and slippers. He carried a stout cane. As Mr. Drew reached the last step, the stranger, who stood in the doorway, commanded, "Don't interfere!"

Nancy's father paid no attention. He turned on the ceiling light in the living room and approached the sofa. At the same moment, Hannah Gruen appeared from the kitchen, also wearing a bathrobe and slippers. In one hand she held a broom, in the other a bucket of water.

Nancy suddenly remembered her pet. Frantically she called out, "Where's Togo?"

"Up in your room waiting for you," Hannah replied. "I shut the door, so he can't get out."

The unfriendly German shepherd had started to back out from under the couch. Hannah whacked him with the broom, and as soon as the dog's head appeared, she threw the bucket of water into his face.

The animal yelped in pain from the whacks, and his owner whistled for him. Willingly, the defeated attacker ran from the house. Ned pushed the sofa forward and hurried after him to the door. The visitors had already left in a car.

The lock had been broken, but with Mr. Drew's help, Ned managed to nail it shut. Then they pushed the sofa back into place.

In the meantime, Nancy had emerged from her hiding place and thanked Hannah for taking care of Togo, who was barking wildly upstairs.

"Shouldn't we report this to the police?" Nancy asked her father. "The dog might be a clue to who the stranger was."

"Yes, that's a good idea. Call right away."

Nancy spoke to the officer on duty and asked if he had a record of large German shepherds owned by the residents of River Heights.

"Yes, we do have a list from the license bureau. I'll phone each owner and find out where his dog has been," he promised. Twenty minutes later he called back. "Every German shepherd in town was indoors during the time when the vicious dog entered your home," he reported.

Nancy thanked the officer and decided that "the voice" and the vicious dog had come from out of town. She mentioned this to her father, and she remarked, "The stranger certainly is well-protected."

Late the next afternoon she and Ned dressed for Moto's farewell party. Since Nancy did not know where Mrs. Rossmeyer's house was, she decided to call Mr. Kikichi.

"Mrs. Rossmeyer is at home?" he inquired, amazed.

"I guess so," Nancy replied. "She invited me

to come and see her. Have you heard from Mr.
Moto?"

"No."

This answer puzzled Nancy, but she did not
tell Mr. Kikichi that the party was supposed to
be in his friend's honor. She got directions and
thanked the man.

On the way to Mrs. Rossmeyer's, Nancy and
Ned discussed the situation. "It's over my head,"
Ned confessed. "Tell me your thoughts."

"There is a possibility Mr. Moto has not been
kidnapped, but instead has chosen to go into
hiding," Nancy said, but she did not sound
convincing.

"But if this is so, why hasn't Mr. Kikichi been
invited to the party?" Ned asked.

"Not only that," Nancy said, "But just before
Mr. Moto disappeared, he told us that he had
never met Mrs. Rossmeyer. If the party is really
in his honor, she must have been introduced to
him after that."

Ned added, "And perhaps he told her about
you. That's why you were invited."

"Could be," Nancy agreed thoughtfully. "But
I still think all this is very strange."

"I do, too," Ned said. "And so does your father.
He gave me a bunch of keys in case Mrs. Rossmeyer is in league with the crooks and tries to
lock us up in her estate." He pulled out two
rings with master keys on them. "You take one,

and I'll take the other. Your Dad felt they might come in handy."

"Good idea." Nancy smiled and put the key ring into her evening bag. "Dad thinks of everything to protect me." She smiled at her companion. "And you do pretty well yourself at the same job." She quickly added, to cover any embarrassment he might feel, "I'm suspicious of those numbers we were told to use for identification. I wonder what it's about."

"I'm with you."

"Suppose I say 'number twelve and escort' to the doorman? I'd like to avoid thirteen."

"That's a good idea," Ned agreed. "And please stay close to me. Together we'll be safer if any funny business is going on."

It was almost dark when they reached the road to which Mr. Kikichi had directed them. It was narrow, rutted, and looked like a lane through the woods, rather than the entrance to an elegant estate.

As they drove along, Ned remarked, "Mrs. Rossmeyer must like privacy, unless Kikichi is sending us in the wrong direction."

Just then, however, the house came into view. Many cars were parked near the brightly lighted entrance.

"He didn't." Nancy chuckled. "And there's really a party going on. Now I feel better."

"So do I," Ned said as he positioned his car in

such a fashion that they could make a quick get-away if necessary. Then the couple walked up to the house.

They could see people through the windows and paused to look at them. About half were American, the other half Asiatic. All wore evening clothes, but many of the outfits were so outlandish that Ned whispered, "They're dressed as if they were going to a Halloween party."

"And look at the jewelry! There must be tons of it!" Nancy said.

She was astonished at the gems the women were wearing. After studying necklaces, Nancy suddenly realized that so far as she could judge from the distance, every one contained twenty-five pearls. Like Mrs. Rossmeyer's stolen piece, there was a large center pearl with twelve smaller ones on each side.

The center pearl differed with each necklace. Some were white, others gray, many were blue, a few were rose-colored, and three of them were black.

Nancy pointed out her discovery to Ned. "There certainly must be some significance to that," she said in a barely audible voice.

"Perhaps we shouldn't go in," Ned suggested. "How about reporting the party to the police? By the way, the man who called you said it was a surprise. Well, I'd say it is!"

Nancy nodded but insisted they go in. "I have

a feeling we're on the verge of making a big discovery, and I don't want to back out now."

He finally agreed, and the two went up a few
steps to a large, open veranda. From there they
walked to the front door. It was opened by a man
in a red velvet uniform. He looked at the couple
and put out an arm as if to stop them.

To allay any suspicion on his part, Nancy
smiled and said, "I am number twelve and this is
my escort."

The doorman stared at her, and she and Ned
held their breaths, wondering what would happen next.

CHAPTER XVIII

The Weird Ceremony

THE doorman at Mrs. Rossmeyer's home did not question Nancy and Ned. They went into a large hall, and from there into the living room where a reception line had formed. Mrs. Rossmeyer was heavily covered with jewelry from head to toe.

Nancy was amazed that she wore no necklace, however. Her white satin dress was covered with gems that sparkled in the artificial light. Even its standing collar and long sleeves were embroidered with numerous pearls, diamonds, rubies, and emeralds.

"She's decked out like a Christmas tree," Ned whispered to Nancy.

The young sleuth suppressed a smile and stared at the woman. She did not look at all like Nancy had pictured her. She was very thin, had prominent cheek bones, and a determined-looking chin. Her hair was straw-colored, and there was an overabundance of rouge on her cheeks.

"I expected her to be beautiful," Nancy said to Ned in a low, disappointed tone.

He grunted almost inaudibly. "She lets her gems make up for her looks!"

Nancy glanced along the receiving line and around the room. She did not see Mr. Moto, the jeweler. "I wonder where he is," the young sleuth thought.

In a few minutes, she and Ned moved up to the head of the receiving line, where Mrs. Rossmeyer was shaking hands with various guests, kissing some, and whispering into one woman's ear.

When Nancy reached the hostess, the girl said, "We appreciate your invitation. Your party is wonderful."

On the spur of the moment she decided not to use her right name. "I'm Nan Drewry," she added, "and this is my friend, Edward Nickson."

Mrs. Rossmeyer stared hard at them but made no comment. She turned to the Japanese man on her left. "I would like you to meet Mr. Moto," she said.

Startled, Nancy shook hands with him and asked, "By any chance are you related to Mr. Moto, the jeweler from River Heights?"

"No, I am not," was the answer.

Ned shook hands with the slightly built man,

but asked no further question. "I hope you enjoy your trip to Japan," he said.

"I am sure I will," Mr. Moto replied, and the couple moved on.

They mingled with the crowd, but realized that they knew no one, and none of the guests spoke to them. So their conversation was confined to admiring the gorgeous paintings, rugs, and tapestries with which the mansion was furnished.

As they walked back into the center hall, Nancy and Ned heard a strange noise upstairs. Curious, they went to the second floor. In one of the beautifully furnished bedrooms, an elderly American woman, dressed in evening attire and wearing a lot of pearl jewelry, was seated on the side of a bed. She rocked back and forth rhythmically, muttering to herself.

She paid no attention when Nancy and Ned walked through the open door. Wondering if the woman were ill and needed help, Nancy went closer. The old lady was mumbling in a sing-song voice.

Ned grabbed Nancy's arm. "She's nuts!" he whispered. "If I were you, I wouldn't get too near her. You never can tell what people like that will do. She may attack you!"

Nancy heeded Ned's warning but listened carefully to the muttering. Finally she managed to distinguish a few words. "Sacred nacre, moon, high tides."

The woman was not only rocking, but rolling her eyes from one side to the other. She repeated the same words over and over and added, "Full moon, beautiful shell, lovely pink."

Nancy whispered to Ned, "These terms were used in ancient times in the pearl cults." Quickly she explained a little about this to him then added, "Maybe this woman belongs to a modern pearl-worshipping cult!"

Ned looked disgusted. "She belongs in a funny farm!"

Nancy hardly paid attention to what he was saying. She wondered if the woman was in a trance, or for some reason, was she acting? The stranger finally stopped muttering and began to moan, her voice rising and falling.

Ned said, "I can't stand any more of this. It's driving me off my rocker!"

Nancy consented to leave. When they walked out of the bedroom, an American man in evening clothes came up to them. He smiled and said, "Mrs. Rossmeyer would like to see you in her private quarters."

Ned hesitated, looking at Nancy. He felt they might be walking into a trap. Nancy nodded almost imperceptably, then started to follow the man. Ned went along reluctantly.

The stranger led them down the long hallway to a door. He clicked on a wall light, then opened the door. Nancy and Ned saw a narrow corridor

in front of them. Did this lead to Mrs. Rossmeyer's private quarters?

The young couple entered the corridor and
the door behind them locked itself. Their guide
suddenly began to sprint toward a door at the far
end of the narrow hall. Before Nancy or Ned
could catch him, he had slipped through the door
and pushed it shut.

Ned tried to open it, but the door was locked.
Then the light in the hallway went out and they
stood in total darkness! Together they groped
their way to the other door. It, too, was locked.

Nancy and Ned were trapped!

For a moment the young people stood motion-
less, thoughts racing through their minds. Suddenly Nancy grabbed her friend's arm. "Ned—
the keys!" she whispered. "Let's try all those keys
Dad gave us."

"That's the best idea you've had all night,"
Ned murmured and pulled out his key ring. As
silently as possible, he tried one key after another. None of them fit!

After he had fumbled with the last one, he
sighed. "That's it. Now let me have yours, and
hope we have better luck!"

Nancy handed him her set, and patiently the
young man tried again. Finally one of the keys
went into the keyhole. Ned maneuvered it carefully, gritting his teeth. Tensely he turned it, but
the key stuck! Ned jiggled it back and forth and

Nancy and Ned were trapped!

then turned it again. This time it worked! He opened the door a crack.

"Wow!" he said, wiping his wet forehead in relief.

The young people tiptoed out into the larger hallway. No one was in sight, but weird-sounding Asiatic music drifted from the first floor. The couple listened for a moment. There were no other sounds.

"What's going on?" Ned asked.

"I don't know, but I mean to find out!" Nancy replied with determination. "It's evident that whatever is taking place, Mrs. Rossmeyer and Mr. Moto didn't want us to see it!"

Carefully Nancy and Ned made their way to the stairs. They saw that no one was in the downstairs hall. Apparently all the guests had assembled in the living room.

The young sleuth stood in silence for a few moments, then motioned for Ned to follow her. Cautiously the two sneaked down the steps to the first landing. From this vantage point they could see everything clearly. Both gasped!

Ned whispered, "I can't believe it!"

In the center of the living room a small red velvet and gold throne had been set up. Mrs. Rossmeyer was seated on it, a pearl tiara on her head. The electric lights had been turned out, and hundreds of candles illuminated the strange scene.

The guests had put on long, white ceremonial robes over their evening clothes and formed a long line. They began marching around Mrs. Rossmeyer. As each one approached her, he or she bowed and then kneeled.

"What do you think this means?" Ned asked Nancy, a puzzled look on his face.

"It's some kind of weird cult," Nancy replied. "I think I know what it is. Tell you later."

Behind the woman seated on the throne stood a Japanese man. He held up a large, purple velvet banner with a beautiful open pink shell painted on it. Attached to one corner was a huge white pearl.

The thought flashed through Nancy's mind, "Could this be the thirteenth pearl stolen from Mr. Moto's shop?"

After the last guest had paid obeisance to Mrs. Rossmeyer, everyone began to dance to the weird music. The performers moaned and cried and rolled their eyes as the woman on the bed had done.

"This is crazy!" Ned declared. "We must call the police!"

Nancy nodded. "Let's get out of here. I hope no one sees us."

The two young people tiptoed down the stairs as fast as they could. Nancy held her breath and kept her eyes on the open living room door, hoping no one would notice them going past.

No one did, and when they reached the front door, the uniformed man was not in sight. Nancy and Ned breathed sighs of relief and slipped quietly out into the darkness.

They ran to Ned's car, and he started it. As he drove along the rutted lane, Nancy put a hand on his right arm.

"Ned, before we notify the police, let's go to the newspaper office!"

CHAPTER XIX

The Thirteenth Pearl

"THE newspaper office?" Ned asked, puzzled.

"Yes," Nancy replied. "I believe that the real Mrs. Rossmeyer is still in Europe and that the one who was at the party is an impostor!"

Ned was amazed. "You mean she just borrowed the house?"

"Yes," Nancy replied.

"I didn't realize that you had never seen a picture of Tanya Rossmeyer," Ned commented.

"Unfortunately I haven't, but the Gazette must have plenty of them."

When they arrived at the newspaper office, a young man at the front counter asked, "You wish to place an ad? It's too late for the morning paper. That has just been put to bed."

Nancy and Ned looked puzzled, and he explained, "That means the forms have been locked in place and the paper put on the press."

Nancy spoke up. "We didn't come about an ad. There may be a big story breaking for you people. May I see some photographs of Mrs. Tanya Rossmeyer?"

The young man, who said to call him Jim, went to an inner room to look through the files. A few minutes later he came back with a folder containing several photographs of the well-known socialite.

"Here she is," Jim said. "I hear the woman's loaded." He grinned. "That means she has a lot of money."

Nancy ignored his facetiousness. After she and Ned had looked at three different photographs of the striking brunette who appeared to be in her late thirties, they were convinced that the woman at the party had indeed been an impostor.

Ned thanked Jim, and the young couple left. When they were outside, Ned remarked, "So that 'goddess' was just a cheap fake!"

"Yes." Suddenly Nancy thought of something else and turned back to the newspaper office. "I wonder if there were any recent articles telling exactly where the real Mrs. Rossmeyer is," she said.

Jim was surprised to see them again. "Did you bring the big story you promised?" he asked.

Nancy smiled. "Not yet. I'd like a little help

first. Will you check recent papers to see if there have been any recent articles about Mrs. Rossmeyer?"

Jim went off and came back with a copy of the morning paper. "Maybe there's something in here," he said.

Nancy and Ned turned the pages and ran their fingers down the various columns. Suddenly Ned stopped.

"Look at this!" he said, and he began to read aloud:

> *Mrs. Tanya Rossmeyer of River Heights is giving a dinner party on Tuesday for Count and Countess Sorrentino.*

Nancy interrupted. "Tuesday! That's today! Where is the item from?"

"Paris," Ned replied.

"That settles it. Mrs. Rossmeyer is in Paris and not in River Heights."

"Is that the big story?" Jim asked.

Once more Nancy smiled enigmatically. "No. But I believe you will have it very soon."

Before the young man could ask further questions, Nancy and Ned raced from the newspaper office. Their next stop was police headquarters. They burst inside and told the officer on duty that a fake Mrs. Rossmeyer had "borrowed" the socialite's home and was having a big and very strange party there.

"What!" the officer said. "I'll get some men with squad cars to investigate at once."

Nancy suggested that the policeman follow her and Ned. "We've just come from the estate and know exactly where it is," she added.

While the men were assembling, Nancy told the officer that she suspected the group who was at the estate were jewel thieves. "They've probably robbed Mrs. Rossmeyer's house. Would you get in touch with my father and Chief McGinnis? I'm sure they'll want to come along."

When the young sleuth and her companion reached the Rossmeyer mansion, they found to their dismay that it was in darkness. The last car of guests was just pulling away. It was not coming toward them, but going out a back service road.

"Let's follow it!" Nancy urged Ned.

"Okay. But we'd better not get too close or the driver will become suspicious."

The chase led beyond the borders of River Heights, and Nancy was worried. Would the police go back now and perhaps notify the State Troopers to continue the hunt?

Nancy said nothing to Ned, but she wished she had brought her own car with its CB radio. Ned had driven his car to her home, and she had seen no reason to make a switch.

After they had traveled a good many miles, the driver ahead turned into a wooded area. The dirt road twisted and turned until it finally led to an encampment. The main house seemed to be a converted barn. For safety, Ned parked some distance away.

He and Nancy jumped out and quietly but quickly hurried forward. They encountered no one, since the people ahead of them had already gone inside. Cautiously the young people went up to the nearest window and peered in.

They recognized many of the people who had been at the party. They were standing around, still in their ceremonial robes, but the scene was not solemn. The cultists were talking and laughing loudly. One of them put on a record, and they began to dance singly or in couples, going through strange gyrations.

Presently two men walked near the window, which was partially open. They were Mr. Kampura and Benny the Slippery One Caputti!

Nancy and Ned dodged out of sight but remained close enough to listen. Benny Caputti laughed raucously. "We certainly pulled that one off all right. Good thing those kids didn't see us and Rosina!"

"That's right," Kampura said. "Praise to the pearl and the lovely moon goddess."

"Say, we brought so much food back, we'd better feed Moto," Benny said.

Kampura chuckled. "Which one?"

"Not our Moto, of course. The sneaky little jeweler who caught on to us and is now sitting in the dungeon!"

"We certainly have to decide what we'll do with him soon. I still think we should have gotten rid of him right away."

Nancy and Ned looked at each other. Mr. Moto the jeweler was the prisoner of the cult people! But where was he, in the house, or one of the other buildings? They wondered if the thieves had harmed him.

Kampura and Caputti were joined by a third man who snickered. "It's a good thing we locked up that girl and her boyfriend. The nerve of them to crash the party!"

The three men moved away from the window, and Nancy whispered to Ned, "They don't even know we've escaped!"

"And they don't know we were invited," Ned added. "I wonder who called you." Nancy admitted she had no idea.

At that moment two other men passed the window and stopped near it. One of them said, "We can't leave that girl and her boyfriend in the hallway forever. Early tomorrow morning, you go back and quietly unlock the doors."

His companion grinned. "And give them some pearl soup!"

Both men laughed uproariously but were interrupted by the "goddess." She reprimanded them for their hilarity and suggested that everyone go to bed.

"There is work to be done in the morning," she declared. "I have a new list of jewelry stores for you to work on."

The woman clapped her hands. Everyone fell silent, and she commanded the cult members to retire to their rooms. Within minutes everyone had left, and the lights were turned out.

Nancy and Ned wondered where the police were. Had the River Heights men forgotten to notify them. Or had the replacements not been able to follow Ned's car?

"Are you game to go inside the house and see if we can find a telephone to notify the police?" Nancy asked.

"Yes. Let's see if we can locate a door that isn't locked."

Not far from where they were standing was an open door. Nancy and Ned tiptoed inside. Before them was a flight of steps with another door at the top. Ned opened it, and they found themselves in a kitchen. It was in darkness, but a small flashlight Nancy pulled from her pocket illuminated their way to another door. It swung open noiselessly, and the two sleuths went into an elegantly furnished dining room.

No telephone was in evidence. Nancy thought, "Perhaps 'Mrs. Rossmeyer' keeps it hidden."

The two young people proceeded through

another door and this time stood stock-still, gaping in astonishment. They were in a small room with a large glass case in the middle of it. It stood on a pedestal, and in the center, swathed in purple velvet, was the form of a woman's neck and shoulders. A light in the top of the case shone on an exquisite pearl necklace draped over the form. Nancy counted the pearls. There were twelve on each side of a huge, magnificent center one with a slightly pinkish cast!

Nancy and Ned were stunned. Was this the one stolen from the real Mrs. Rossmeyer? Was it the one her companion had brought to Mr. Moto for repairs?

In front of the glass case, three figures in white hooded robes were kneeling on the floor. They remained in that position and gave no indication that they had seen or heard the young people. Every few seconds they glanced up at the necklace with adoring eyes.

Nancy put her lips to Ned's ear. "We *must* get the police!"

The two retraced their steps through the dining room and kitchen and went outside.

"Maybe the officers lost us and couldn't find this place," Ned suggested. "Why don't we walk up the road and wave them down?"

Nancy agreed, and they started off. As they hurried along the dirt road, they were suddenly stopped by two men who appeared from the bushes and blocked their way like huge, looming shadows!

Nancy and Ned stood frozen to the spot. Before they had a chance to think, they were tackled by the two men. As the young couple fought desperately, they smelled a strong, sweet odor coming from cloths that their attackers had shoved in their faces. Nancy and Ned blacked out!

CHAPTER XX

The Captive's Story

SOME time later, Nancy revived. She was lying on a hard, cold floor in total darkness.

Relieved that she was neither bound nor gagged, she sat up. "Ned?" she called out. "Ned, are you here?"

Ned tried to clear his head of the confusion resulting from his ordeal. "I'm here," he replied. "Where are you?"

Nancy felt in her pocket for the flashlight. Fortunately it had not been taken from her. She played the beam around. "I think we're in a barn," she said, "and—"

A low groan interrupted her. It came from a prone figure lying near Nancy. The young people rushed up to the bound and gagged victim, and Nancy shone her light on him.

"Mr. Moto!" she cried out in dismay.

Quickly Nancy and Ned unbound the jeweler and removed the cloth from his mouth. "Are you all right?" Nancy asked anxiously.

"Much better now that the gag is off," the man replied. As Nancy and Ned raised him to a sitting position, a smile crossed his face. "Miss Drew!" he exclaimed. "How did you find me? And who is this young man?"

"This is my friend Ned Nickerson. But before we tell you anything more, we must get away from here."

"How did you come in here?" Mr. Moto asked. "I was asleep and didn't hear anyone enter."

"We were taken prisoners," Nancy replied ruefully, "and gassed."

"Oh, dear!" Mr. Moto cried out. "Then we will not be able to leave. The big doors are padlocked on the outside."

Ned, who had gone to investigate, came to the same conclusion. "He's right, Nancy. There's no way to get these open."

"We'll figure out something," Nancy said, trying to sound calm. "In the meantime, Mr. Moto, tell us what happened to you."

"I found out about the cult and the jewel thieves, so they kidnapped me. Mr. Kampura did it. He left his sandals by mistake and was quite worried that they would be found."

"We did find them," Nancy said. "And we

suspected they belonged to him, but we couldn't prove it."

Mr. Moto nodded. "In order to avoid any suspicion," he went on, "they made me call my friend Mr. Kikichi and ask him to take over the store while I was supposedly in Japan."

"Then Mr. Kikichi is innocent after all!" Ned exclaimed.

"Of course he is," Mr. Moto said. "Do you know if he's all right?"

"Yes," Nancy replied. "I'm afraid he was hurt when your store was burglarized after your disappearance, but he's fine now."

"Oh, dear, oh—" Mr. Moto clasped his hands in despair and turned white. Nancy was afraid he might have another attack, but she and Ned managed to calm the jeweler.

"Please don't worry," Nancy told him. "Mr. Kikichi has recovered completely, and I'm sure we're close to solving this mystery, and you will be able to recover your losses."

"Tell us what happened to you after you were brought here," Ned urged.

"They held me in this barn and only unbound me long enough so I could eat and get some exercise. When I talked to you on the telephone, Miss Drew—"

"It was *you* who called and invited me to Mrs. Rossmeyer's party?" Nancy asked, very surprised.

"Yes, it was. The man who comes in here to watch me while I'm eating was called away on an emergency for a few minutes. I know there is a phone in the covered box over in that corner, so I used it."

"That was clever and very courageous," Nancy said admiringly.

"But why didn't you tell Nancy you were a prisoner?" Ned inquired.

"I was afraid that someone might overhear me on an extension. I am sure there are many phones in the complex here. That is why I disguised my voice and did not ask for help directly or tell you to go to the police. I thought you would catch on and try to rescue me."

"But how did you know about the party?" Nancy asked.

"I overheard two men say they were using Mrs. Rossmeyer's house for a big ceremonial celebration. They expected an honored guest whose name happens to be Moto, too. He was on his way to Japan."

"We met him," Nancy said.

"He is a close friend of the woman who calls herself Mrs. Rossmeyer," Mr. Moto went on, "and works as a liaison between this country and Japan. The fake Mrs. Rossmeyer is an expert jewel thief and organizes those who do the stealing for the Caputti gang."

"Are all the cult members thieves?" Ned asked.

"Not all. Only a select group. The others are dedicated pearl cultists."

"We must get out of here!" Nancy said after a moment of silence. "Can't we break down the door, Ned?"

"That would make so much noise we'd attract their attention, and they'd come running," he objected. "We'll have to think of something else."

At this moment they heard a loud commotion at the main house. Through a crack in the door, they could see lights flashing and orders being issued.

"The police have arrived!" Nancy exclaimed, relieved.

"If you're right," Ned said, "then we may as well try to break down the door!"

He looked around for a pole or another heavy article they could use as a battering ram. He found several new wooden fence rails and picked one up. It was very heavy. Ned took hold of the front end, Nancy grabbed the middle, and Mr. Moto insisted upon holding the rear.

Wham! The barn doors shivered but did not break. The three retreated a little, then ran forward into the wooden barrier again. This time there was a splintering crash.

"Once more!" Ned urged.

They went back farther, then rushed ahead

and with great force, rammed the door. The lock broke away, and the doors flew open.

The prisoners dashed out. Lights from cars and lanterns proved that the police had surrounded the house. Cultists in slippers and bathrobes were running from several exits, screaming and calling on the pearl goddess.

Nancy, Ned, and Mr. Moto hurried toward the house. The jeweler panted. "Crazy thieves!"

They found the place bustling with police. Many of the cultists had already been rounded up, including Mr. Kampura, Benny the Slippery One Caputti, and the "pearl goddess." She was being questioned along with the other Mr. Moto.

The officer in charge told her that all of them were under arrest, but the woman argued violently. In an arrogant manner she kept proclaiming her innocence, insisting that the cult was only interested in tranquility. Suddenly she noticed Mr. Moto, the jeweler, and blanched.

He cried out angrily, "I accuse you of kidnapping me and holding me prisoner, and of impersonating Mrs. Rossmeyer!"

The woman stared at him, speechless.

Nancy stepped forward. "You had me and my escort locked in Mrs. Rossmeyer's home tonight!"

Before the woman had a chance to reply, there was loud barking outside, then a policeman came in, desperately trying to contain a fierce German shepherd that bounded up to Mr. Caputti, pulling the officer along.

"That's the vicious dog that almost attacked us at my home after his owner broke the door down!" Nancy cried out. "And you were the one who sent me those warning notes in Tokyo!" She pointed at Benny the Slippery One, who glared at her in silence.

Two more prisoners were brought in, a heavy-set blond woman who struggled fiercely and a young Japanese man.

"Rosina Caputti!" Nancy exclaimed. "She managed to get out of the Tokyo prison with the help of Mr. Kampura and a number of forged documents! And that man next to her stole a pearl necklace from Mr. Moto's shop and made his getaway just when my girl friends and I arrived."

The officer in charge looked at Nancy admiringly. "You seem to know more about these people than we do. Would you be willing to testify against them?"

"Yes, indeed," Nancy replied.

Mr. Moto spoke up. "While you are busy rounding up these criminals, I would like permission to search this house. I am sure I can identify many stolen pieces of jewelry. From conversations I overheard, I know where some of their hiding places are."

"Go ahead," the officer told him, and Mr. Moto,

Nancy, and Ned started off. The girl sleuth first led Mr. Moto to the room where the priceless necklace was displayed in the glass case.

Excitedly he rushed up and examined the piece. "It is the one, the very one, that was stolen from me! The one Mrs. Rossmeyer left in my care!"

Mr. Moto took the lid off the glass case and reached in. With almost loving hands he lifted the necklace from the figure, gazed at it, and dropped it into his pocket.

"I am so thankful to get it back," he said, "and Nancy Drew deserves full credit for finding this."

Nancy blushed at the praise. "I had plenty of help—my girl friends, my father, and Ned, to say nothing of Professor Mise and his wonderful relatives in Tokyo."

"You went to Tokyo?"

"Yes. My father and I stayed with the professor's brother and his wife. While I was there, I tried to find your brother, Tetsuo, because I thought he might be able to tell me where you were. But he had moved, and none of the neighbors knew his new address."

"How did you know I had a brother? You are an incredible detective."

"Mrs. Rooney, your neighbor, told me."

Mr. Moto smiled. "She is a nice lady. I talk to her often. And you are right. Tetsuo moved to a small town near Kyoto. In a way, I am glad you did not find him. He knew nothing about my problems, of course, and if he had any idea of my disappearance, I am sure he would have been very worried."

Nancy nodded. "So it all turned out for the best. Now we'd better continue searching this house."

In their hunt, the trio found most of the pieces that had been stolen from Mr. Moto's shop while Nancy and her father were in Japan.

"This proves that the cultists were responsible for that robbery," Nancy said, "and for harming Mr. Kikichi."

Mr. Moto pulled open a secret drawer in a desk that he had heard Kampura mention to another member of the cult, and he pulled out many strings of pearls. Each one had a thirteenth pearl in the middle!

"Look how beautiful they are!" Mr. Moto said. "All different hues. I wonder where these came from?"

"There have been many thefts, especially in Japan," Nancy said. "I'm sure the pieces can eventually be identified and returned to their rightful owners."

Her next find was a diamond and ruby necklace. "That's like the one that was slipped into my kimono sleeve to make me look like a thief!" she said.

"Where did that happen?" Mr. Moto asked, taken aback.

"At a wedding in Tokyo."

The jeweler threw up his hands. "It is true that World Wide Gems have dishonest people working in every country!"

"I'm afraid so," Nancy answered. "No doubt this will come out at the trial."

"I wonder who the leader of the group is," Nancy mused.

"Mr. Kampura. I overheard someone say this. He has confederates all over the world who are giving World Wide Gems a bad name."

"What about the real Mrs. Rossmeyer?" Nancy asked. "She's on the board of directors of that company, you know."

"I was not aware of that. But I do know she is a fine, honest lady. Just before she left for Europe, Mrs. Rossmeyer had me appraise a lot of her jewelry. They are among the pieces we found."

At this moment Mr. Drew and Chief McGinnis walked into the room. The lawyer grabbed his daughter affectionately.

"Thank goodness you're safe!" he said. Then his eyes fell on the jeweler. "Mr. Moto!" he exclaimed. "I'm so glad to see you. Where have you been?"

"Tied up in the barn. Nancy and Ned saved me from a terrible fate," Mr. Moto replied. "I must make charges against my kidnappers and the other jewel thieves. Will you represent me?"

The lawyer said he would be very glad to do so. Together the men walked into the room where the "pearl goddess" was still arguing with police about her innocence.

Mr. Drew said to her, "How do you explain your connection with World Wide Gems, Inc.?"

At first the woman would not admit anything, but finally, seeing that her protests were useless, she broke down and told the full story.

The heads of World Wide Gems, Inc. were honest men, but many of those under them in various countries were committing thefts under the supervision of Mr. Kampura. They also employed groups of thieves and used the cultist organization to cover up the operation and their encampment as a place to hide their loot.

After all the guilty parties had been taken away by the police, Nancy and Ned drove off in his car to return to River Heights.

"Nancy, you did a great job," he praised her as he drove down the wooded lane.

She merely smiled and said, "You were a terrific help, Ned." She paused a moment, then said, "Do you think we'll ever get another mystery to solve?"

Ned chuckled. "Knowing you, I would say you'll find one in no time."

Ned's prediction was to come true soon when Nancy would start working on *The Triple Hoax*.

Mr. Drew had offered to take Mr. Moto to his home. On the way, the Japanese jeweler said to him, "I think you have the most wonderful daughter in the world!"

ORDER FORM

NANCY DREW MYSTERY STORIES®

by Carolyn Keene

Now that you've met Nancy Drew, we're sure you'll want to read the thrilling adventures in the *Nancy Drew Mystery Stories®*.

To make it easy for you to own all the books in this action-packed series, we've enclosed this handy order form.

56 TITLES AT YOUR BOOKSELLER OR COMPLETE THIS HANDY COUPON AND MAIL TO:

GROSSET & DUNLAP, INC.
P.O. Box 941, Madison Square Post Office, New York, N.Y. 10010

Please send me the *Nancy Drew Mystery Stories®* checked below @$2.95 each, plus 50¢ *per book* postage and handling. My check or money order for $_____ is enclosed. (Please do not send cash.)

☐	1.	Secret of the Old Clock	9501-7	☐	29.	Mystery at the Ski Jump	9529-7
☐	2.	Hidden Staircase	9502-5	☐	30.	Clue of the Velvet Mask	9530-0
☐	3.	Bungalow Mystery	9503-3	☐	31.	Ringmaster's Secret	9531-9
☐	4.	Mystery at Lilac Inn	9504-1	☐	32.	Scarlet Slipper Mystery	9532-7
☐	5.	Secret of Shadow Ranch	9505-X	☐	33.	Witch Tree Symbol	9533-5
☐	6.	Secret of Red Gate Farm	9506-8	☐	34.	Hidden Window Mystery	9534-3
☐	7.	Clue in the Diary	9507-6	☐	35.	Haunted Showboat	9535-1
☐	8.	Nancy's Mysterious Letter	9508-4	☐	36.	Secret of the Golden Pavilion	9536-X
☐	9.	The Sign of the Twisted Candles	9509-2	☐	37.	Clue in the Old Stagecoach	9537-8
☐	10.	Password to Larkspur Lane	9510-6	☐	38.	Mystery of the Fire Dragon	9538-6
☐	11.	Clue of the Broken Locket	9511-4	☐	39.	Clue of the Dancing Puppet	9539-4
☐	12.	The Message in the Hollow Oak	9512-2	☐	40.	Moonstone Castle Mystery	9540-8
☐	13.	Mystery of the Ivory Charm	9513-0	☐	41.	Clue of the Whistling Bagpipes	9541-6
☐	14.	The Whispering Statue	9514-9	☐	42.	Phantom of Pine Hill	9542-4
☐	15.	Haunted Bridge	9515-7	☐	43.	Mystery of the 99 Steps	9543-2
☐	16.	Clue of the Tapping Heels	9516-5	☐	44.	Clue in the Crossword Cipher	9544-0
☐	17.	Mystery of the Brass Bound Trunk	9517-3	☐	45.	Spider Sapphire Mystery	9545-9
				☐	46.	The Invisible Intruder	9546-7
☐	18.	Mystery at Moss-Covered Mansion	9518-1	☐	47.	The Mysterious Mannequin	9547-5
				☐	48.	The Crooked Banister	9548-3
☐	19.	Quest of the Missing Map	9519-X	☐	49.	The Secret of Mirror Bay	9549-1
☐	20.	Clue in the Jewel Box	9520-3	☐	50.	The Double Jinx Mystery	9550-5
☐	21.	The Secret in the Old Attic	9521-1	☐	51.	Mystery of the Glowing Eye	9551-3
☐	22.	Clue in the Crumbling Wall	9522-X	☐	52.	The Secret of the Forgotten City	9552-1
☐	23.	Mystery of the Tolling Bell	9523-8				
☐	24.	Clue in the Old Album	9524-6	☐	53.	The Sky Phantom	9553-X
☐	25.	Ghost of Blackwood Hall	9525-4	☐	54.	The Strange Message in the Parchment	9554-8
☐	26.	Clue of the Leaning Chimney	9526-2				
☐	27.	Secret of the Wooden Lady	9527-0	☐	55.	Mystery of Crocodile Island	9555-6
☐	28.	The Clue of the Black Keys	9528-9	☐	56.	The Thirteenth Pearl	9556-4

SHIP TO:

NAME _____
(please print)

ADDRESS _____

CITY _____ STATE _____ ZIP _____

Printed in U.S.A. **Please do not send cash.**